Also by Trae Dorn

The Mia Graves Series
The Witch and the Rose
Bloody Damn Rite
Shadowcasting
Buried Memories
The Perfect Host

Peregrine Lake Series
(with art by Ethan Flanagan)
Welcome to Peregrine Lake

Other Comics and Graphic Novels
UnCONventional
The Chronicles of Crosarth

Mia Graves Book One

THE WITCH AND THE ROSE

TRAE DORN

NERD &TIE

www.nerdandtie.com
www.traedorn.com

For Crysta,
who thankfully still puts up
with my witchy nonsense.

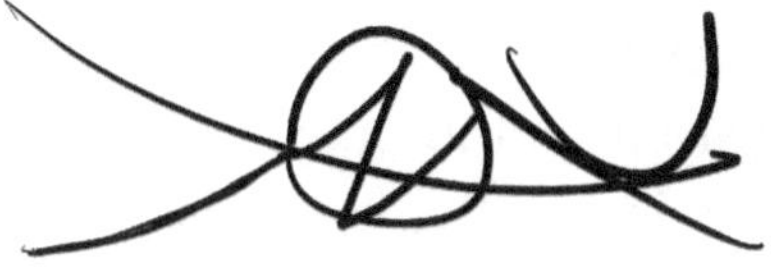

Prologue

A cold wind howled at the window. Autumn had set its teeth into the early evening, and wasn't letting go.

Lila stood in front of the mirror in her well appointed bedroom. She smoothed the deep red silk of her dress and smiled quietly at her reflection. Satisfied with the way the garment hung on her slender frame, she sat down at the ornate vanity and fixed her short dark hair. With practiced care, she made sure not a strand was out of place. The light's flickered around her, casting an ethereal glow on her pale skin as she carefully applied crimson lipstick.

Father really does need someone to look at the wiring in this house, she thought. The flickering was happening more often these days. It was a grand house, likely the largest in their small Indiana town, but it had been built in the 1800s. The electrical wiring was a later addition, and it seemed to be constantly acting up.

"Tonight is going to be aces," she whispered to herself, and excitement bubbled up through her like champagne. It was the perfect evening for a night out on the town. Harold was going to take her out for a lovely dinner, and then they'd find some hole in the wall club to meet up with friends after to see some live music and dance the evening away.

As she fastened a simple gold necklace around her neck, her thoughts drifted to her impending freedom. She'd be married soon, and she and Harold could start their life outside of the microscope that defined their world in Parrish Mills. Harold had already bought them a house in Chicago, and the idea of a big city where every move wasn't the subject of small town gossip excited Lila to no end.

Her future finally held so many possibilities, and she couldn't wait to meet it.

A sudden noise from the hallway snapped Lila back to reality. It was like something heavy had been roughly dropped on the floor. Lila's pulse quickened, and she held her breath, straining to listen for any other sounds. Father was out of town on business, and she had given the staff the night off. It was too early for Harold to arrive, and he would have rung the bell.

No one should be in the house but her.

Her maid, Mary, had only left half an hour ago. Maybe she'd forgotten something and come back? Lila hoped desperately this was the case.

"Mary?" Lila called out, her voice wavering, betraying her growing unease. "Is that you?"

Silence greeted her, which only amplified the sense of foreboding that slithered up her spine like a serpent. She knew she should remain in the safety of her room, but curiosity gnawed at her like a ravenous beast. And so, against her better judgment, Lila stood and walked to her door.

"Mary!" she called again, more forcefully this time, as she placed one tentative foot outside her bedroom door. "You better not be playing any tricks on me!"

But the hallway remained eerily quiet. It's cold, still air did nothing but make the feeling of dread in the pit of her stomach grow. The shadows seemed to cling to her like tendrils of darkness, her heightened senses prickling with the unmistakable sense that she was not alone.

"Come on, Lila," she muttered under her breath, her heart pounding in her chest. "It's just the house settling. Or perhaps a raccoon got into the attic. You're letting your imagination run wild."

Even as she tried to reassure herself though, Lila couldn't shake the feeling that something sinister lurked just beyond the threshold of her perception, waiting for the perfect moment to strike.

With a deep breath, Lila steeled herself and stepped into the darkened hallway. The shadows seemed to writhe and pulsate around her, as if alive with some malevolent intent. She clutched at the fabric of her red silk dress, her fingers trembling with both fear and determination. Her footsteps echoed through the empty corridor, each sound magnified by the oppressive silence that followed.

"Mary?" she called again, her voice barely more than a whisper. "If you're here, please answer me."

But all that greeted her was an unforgiving void, swallowing her words and leaving her feeling more isolated than ever before. Despite the chill in the air, beads of sweat gathered on her forehead and her heart beat fast like a drummer on a roll.

As she stood in the hallway, she hesitated, wavering between the desire to confront whatever awaited her and the instinct to flee back to the safety of her room. With one last desperate call for Mary, Lila stepped back into her room, praying that the familiar sanctuary would offer some semblance of security.

"Mary, please, I need-"

Her words died in her throat as she caught sight of the dark figure standing in her bedroom. It was like a man born of smoke, roiling like a storm before her. Terror gripped her chest like icy fingers, squeezing the very air from her lungs. She began to panic, and tried run, but the door to the room slammed closed in front of her.

"Who are you?" she managed to choke out, her voice barely audible. "What do you want?"

The figure remained silent, its presence casting a shadow over the room that seemed to consume every flicker of hope and reason. Lila's mind raced, torn between her desire for answers and the primal need to escape the nightmare that had invaded her once-safe haven.

"Please," she whispered, her voice trembling with fear and desperation. "Just let me go."

Lila's legs wavered beneath her, threatening to buckle at any moment as the dark figure loomed closer. The air in the room seemed to thicken, suffocating her with an oppressive weight she couldn't escape. She forced herself to take a shaky step backward, her body begging for flight despite the paralyzing fear that held her captive.

"Anna!" the figure screamed in an unearthly voice, its tone both chilling and guttural. "Did you really think you could leave me!"

"Who are you?" Lila cried out, her confusion battling against the terror that threatened to drown her. "Who's Anna? Please, just let me go!"

"Anna! You belong to me!" The figure's words reverberated through the room like an ominous thunderclap, a menacing echo of rage and hatred.

Desperate to evade the entity's grasp, Lila lunged for the door, her fingers fumbling for the handle. As she tried to pry it open, she found it impossible to move.

"Please," she begged, her knuckles white as she tried to force the door open. "I'm not who you think I am!"

"Anna, my sweet daughter," it whispered, "You know what happened when your mother tried to leave. You know what I have to do."

"Stop calling me Anna!" Lila shouted, her frustration mounting as the door refused to budge. "You've got the wrong person! My name is Lila, and you are not my father!"

"Escape is futile, Anna." The figure's voice was once again laced with a sinister edge. "And I will make sure you never leave me."

Lila watched the figure move towards her, her back against the door.

Freedom would always remain out of reach.

Chapter 1

Riley Whittaker stood at the front of her political science class, chalk dust clinging to the tips of her fingers as she finished scribbling the last points on the blackboard. Her straight, long blonde hair was pulled back into a tight ponytail, accentuating the sharp angles of her face and the fierce determination in her blue eyes.

"So the counterpoint to that in international relations is realism," she told her students with a warm yet authoritative voice, "When we're contrasting these ideas, it's much more important to remember that they're less a reflection of how the world objectively works, and more so the attitudes and biases of the people acting on behalf of the state."

In the two years that she'd been an associate professor at Garrity University, Riley had gained a reputation for her intelligence, compassion, and strong sense of curiosity. She took pride in fostering critical thinking among her students and encouraging them to dig deeper into the subjects they studied.

Well, at least among the ones who actually showed up for class.

But while she thrived in the academic world, her personal life was best described as "a massive garbage fire." Just weeks before their wedding, her fiancé Jake had unceremoniously dumped her, leaving her devastated and longing for a fresh start. The emotional damage was still raw, making her feel vulnerable and exposed like an open wound in need of stitches.

"Professor Whittaker?" A soft-spoken student interrupted her thoughts, causing Riley to snap back to reality.

"Uh, yes?" She replied, refocusing on the present.

"What exactly is the difference between realism and neorealism?"

"Realism is driven by beliefs about human nature, while neorealism is more focused on a state's place in the international system – both are preferred by the deeply selfish and stupid," she said with a smirk, launching into a detailed explanation. She could probably do this lecture in her sleep, which was good because Riley was definitely running on autopilot.

Despite her best efforts, she kept thinking about Jake. Their wedding was supposed to be this weekend. It had been hell canceling the venue, band, food, and twenty billion other things. Beyond the lost deposits and nonrefundable fees, the humiliation of telling her whole family out west had been an ordeal.

Riley could already picture the look of pity on her mother's face when she came home for Thanksgiving alone in a couple of months.

"Alright, that's it for today," she announced once the lecture had come to an end, shaking off the lingering melancholy. "Don't forget to read the assigned chapters, and I'll see you all Thursday."

As the students filed out of the room, Riley felt a strange sense of emptiness settling in her chest. She thought she and Jake were building a life together. They'd even bought an old house with the promise of fixing it up and starting a family. None of that was going to happen now. Jake was back in Chicago with his brother, and Riley was here.

Alone.

Riley had wasted too many years of her life on Jake Darrow, and she wasn't getting them back. She hated that he was gone, she hated that she missed him, and she just… hated *him*. She needed to blow off steam. She needed to do something reckless

Riley was desperate for a distraction.

****

The moment Riley stepped into The Drunken Siren, she felt a sense of relief wash over her like a tidal wave. The bar was a familiar haven, an escape from the turmoil of her life and the perfect place to forget about Jake – if only for an hour or two. The dimly lit room buzzed with the hum of conversation and laughter, while the neon signs cast a kaleidoscope of colors onto the dark wooden floors.

"Hey there, Riley!" called out the bartender, Sam, as he polished a glass behind the counter. He was a tall man in his late thirties with a crooked smile that never quite reached his eyes. He'd been working at the bar for as long as Riley had been coming in, and their friendship had grown over the years through a mutual appreciation for whiskey and sarcasm.

Though Riley suspected the reason Sam *actually* liked her was because she was a decent tipper.

"Sam," Riley replied, returning his nod as she slid onto a worn leather barstool. "Maker's Mark neat, please."

"Rough day?" he asked, already reaching for her favorite bottle.

"Let's just say that by the end of the night I don't want to remember my own name," she answered, her eyes glinting with unhealthy determination.

Riley winced a little as Sam dropped ice cubes into a glass. At some point she was going to have to explain to a grown man how to do his job correctly and not screw up her incredibly simple drink order, but tonight was not that night. As Sam poured her drink, Riley lost herself in the swirls of amber liquid, watching as it cascaded over the ice before settling into a pool of temporary solace. She raised the glass to her lips, inhaling the rich aroma before allowing the fiery burn of the whiskey to slide down her throat. With each sip, she let go of her heartache and frustration, bit by bit, until the world around her became nothing more than a blur of sounds and colors.

"Hey, don't drown your sorrows too much, Riley," Sam warned gently, placing a hand on her shoulder. "Don't want you to kill too many brain cells."

"Thanks, Sam," she said, forcing a smile. "But sometimes intelligence can't compete with the need to feel numb."

"Fair enough," he conceded, stepping away to tend to another customer.

Riley continued to sip her whiskey, allowing herself to become swallowed up by the lively atmosphere of the bar. The weight of her sadness began to lift, if only slightly, as the music and laughter swirled around her like a comforting blanket. She was grateful for the temporary reprieve from reality – even if it wouldn't last forever.

"Go fuck yourself, Jake," she whispered to herself, raising her glass in a silent toast before downing the rest of her drink in one fiery gulp.

As the warmth of the whiskey continued to spread through Riley's veins, her gaze wandered over the bustling room. Her eyes landed on a figure across the bar, and she instantly felt drawn to her. The woman was beautiful, with long, curly black hair cascading down her back, framing a face that held a captivating mix of amusement and mystery. She was laughing at something another patron said, her dark brown eyes sparkling with mischief.

"Who's that?" Riley asked Sam, trying to sound casual as she nodded toward the stranger.

"Her? I think her name's Mia something? Mia Graves, maybe?" he replied. "Don't know much about her, but she's been coming in the last few weeks. Bit of a mystery, honestly. She certainly catches people's attention."

Riley's curiosity piqued as she stared at Mia from across the bar. What drew her eye the most were the intricate tattoos adorning Mia's skin. They seemed to weave a story of their own, snaking up her arms, dancing across her shoulders, and disappearing beneath the hem of her low-cut top and re-emerged on her thighs under her skirt. They were unlike anything Riley had seen before. The looked like the kind of arcane runes and symbols you'd see in a fantasy or horror film, which Riley would normally find a little cheesy, but they seemed to hold an almost otherworldly energy.

"Her tattoos are... incredible," Riley murmured, unable to tear her eyes away from the mesmerizing designs.

"Yep, she's got quite the collection," Sam agreed, polishing a glass absentmindedly. "Makes you curious where she got them done."

"It would be something to ask her" Riley said to herself. There was something undeniably magnetic about Mia, the way she moved, the way the corner of her mouth crept up into a smile while she talked, The way she held herself in conversation which somehow made her seem both commanding and vulnerable. It was like she had an aura that called out to Riley in a way she couldn't quite explain.

"Ask her anything you'd like," Sam said with a shrug. "Let me know if you get any answers. The regulars have been talking about her nonstop. She's almost become a bit of a legend."

Riley found herself captivated by Mia, her imagination running wild as she involuntarily traced the path of the tattoos snaking under Mia's short skirt in her mind. A sense of excitement, mixed with a hint of danger, coursed through her, and she felt that inexplicable urge to know more about this mysterious woman.

"Maybe I should go introduce myself," Riley mused, the whiskey-fueled courage urging her on.

"Couldn't hurt," Sam encouraged with a grin. "I'll have another drink ready for you if it all goes wrong, okay?

"Thanks for the vote of confidence, Sam," Riley replied sarcastically, rolling her eyes as she took a deep breath and started making her way across the room.

As Riley approached Mia, her nerves almost started to get the better of her. Mia was probably the most attractive woman she'd ever seen. With every step closer, her heartbeat quickened. She hadn't approached someone like this since undergrad, but when you're at the bottom already, you don't really have anywhere to fall.

"Hey there," Riley said smoothly, her voice just barely betraying her nervousness. "I could use some help picking out my next drink."

Mia glanced up from her own glass, her dark eyes seeming to drink in all of Riley. Mia leaned forward, a lock of her long curly hair falling in front of her eyes. "Sure thing. What are you in the mood for?"

"Something... adventurous," Riley replied, matching Mia's grin with one of her own. "I've had enough of the usual lately." Riley was doing her best to flirt, but she was incredibly out of practice. On the upside, Mia seemed to be picking up on what was happening, which provided at least *some* modicum of relief.

"Adventurous, huh?" Mia's voice was like smoke on a crisp autumn breeze, and as Riley watched the way her black curls danced around her shoulders she felt a shiver of anticipation race down her spine. "How about a Gravedigger? It's got a bit of a kick to it."

"Sounds perfect," Riley agreed, her heart pounding with equal parts excitement and fear at the prospect of diving into uncharted territory. She had no idea what that drink was (and she was sure Sam would hand her something that barely resembled what it was supposed to be), but taking a risk seemed like the right call. As Sam prepared their drinks, she allowed herself to get lost in the conversation, her mind occasionally wandering to the thought of tracing those tattoos with her own fingers.

"Cheers," Mia said, raising her glass as they clinked them together. The moment their gazes locked, Riley felt a surge of electricity pass through her. She had almost forgotten what flirting with a stranger felt like.

"My name's Riley. From what my friend Sam says you're Mia? You've become a bit of a legend around here apparently," Riley ventured, curiosity getting the better of her. "All these tattoos, they must have some incredible stories behind them."

Mia raised an eyebrow, her lips curling in amusement. "A legend? I only moved to Indiana from Boston three weeks ago and I'm already a legend. And the tattoos are a story unto themselves... I've lived *unconventionally* to say the least."

"Unconventional is just what I need right now," Riley admitted, emboldened by the alcohol and her growing attraction to Mia. She bit her lip, unsure if she was crossing a line, but desperate to find out what lay on the other side. "I don't suppose you'd be willing to share some of those stories with me?"

"Maybe," Mia teased, her voice low and sultry as she leaned closer. "But first, you'll have to tell me something about yourself that nobody else knows. A secret, if you will."

Feeling reckless and alive in a way she couldn't remember experiencing in a very long time, Riley took a deep breath and let the truth tumble from her lips. "When I was in college, I stole a police horse. Rode it around town topless. Never got caught."

"Interesting," Mia murmured, her dark eyes twinkling with intrigue. "You might be a bit less buttoned up than the gray pantsuit leads on, Riley."

"If the clothes make me seem buttoned up, you could always try unbuttoning them," Riley whispered into Mia's ear.

"You know, Riley, I think we're going to get along just fine," Mia replied with a grin.

As they continued to talk and flirt, Riley's infatuation with Mia kept growing stronger. A little touch here, a small smile there – the enigmatic woman drew her like a moth to a flame. The night progressed quickly, and before Riley knew it, she found herself standing in the dimly lit parking lot of Mia's building, her apartment opening directly to the outside. The contrast between the bar's lively atmosphere and the quiet intimacy of the quiet night was striking. As Mia unlocked her door, Riley couldn't help but feel a thrill of anticipation and excitement at what lay ahead.

"Welcome to my humble abode," Mia said with a grin, opening the door to reveal a small studio apartment. It was cozy and inviting, romantically lit with eclectic decor that seemed to reflect the mystery surrounding Mia.

"Wow, it's cute," Riley breathed as she stepped inside, curiosity and desire swirling within her. She tried to take in all the unique trinkets and knick knacks adorning the walls but found her attention drawn back to Mia, who stood directly in front of her.

"That's certainly a way to describe it," Mia replied, smirking. "I know it's not much space, but I make the most of it." She moved closer, the warmth radiating from her body intoxicating. "Now, where were we?"

"Before we were so rudely interrupted by bar close?" Riley teased, nerves temporarily dissipating. Mia's presence seemed to have a calming effect on her, even as her heart raced with anticipation.

"Ah, yes," Mia chuckled, gently cupping Riley's face in her hands. "Right here."

Riley felt a thrill run through her as their lips met for the first time. The kiss was soft and tender, but held an intensity that belied the roiling fire simmering just below the surface. Their bodies pressed together, and Riley reveled in the sensation of their closeness. Mia's hands began to slide under Riley's clothes, exploring and igniting a passion within her that she didn't know she possessed.

"God, Mia, I need this," Riley gasped when they broke apart momentarily. "I need to forget everything else and just be here, with you."

"Then let me take care of you," Mia whispered, her voice low and seductive. "Let yourself go and trust me."

Riley nodded, a mixture of excitement and vulnerability washing over her as she allowed herself to be led to the small bed that sat against one side of the studio apartment. She closed her eyes, focusing on the sensation of Mia's fingers tracing intricate patterns over her skin, the heat of her body pressed against her own.

Mia took her time slowly removing Riley's clothes, discarding each piece one by one. She gently pushed Riley back onto the bed, and began to pull off her own. Riley marveled at the sight of Mia's tattoos, which now seemed to glow in the dim light of the room. Riley knew it must be a trick of the light, but it made Mia's beauty almost ethereal.

Mia's touch was electric, and Riley found herself gasping for breath as they moved together, lost in a whirlwind of passion and desire. It was reckless and wild, unlike anything she'd experienced in a very long time, and she couldn't help but crave more.

"God yes, please," Riley pleaded, her body aching for more contact, more connection. She needed to feel alive, to forget the pain and heartache that had consumed her lately.

"Anything for you," Mia murmured, her fingers expertly finding every sensitive spot, every hidden secret that Riley didn't even know she had. The pleasure was intense, almost overwhelming, but Riley refused to hold back, determined to embrace this unexpected encounter and everything it offered.

And as they finally collapsed together, sweat-slicked and sated, Riley knew that this night – this single, reckless moment of abandon – was something she'd never forget.

****

The first light of dawn crept through the tattered curtains that hung over the apartment's single window, casting thin beams of sunlight across Riley's face as she lay tangled in sweat-soaked sheets. She blinked against the invading brightness, her mind still heavy with sleep and the lingering haze of whiskey. Beside her, Mia's chest rose and fell with the steady rhythm of deep slumber, her long black hair splayed like a halo around her beautiful, mysterious face.

"Shit," Riley whispered to herself, her heart sinking as reality came crashing down upon her. The night before had been wild, exhilarating, and utterly unlike anything she had ever experienced – but now, in the cold light of day, it felt like a terrible mistake.

She wasn't ready for this. She hadn't been with anyone except Jake in so long. Why did she think this would be a good idea?

Untangling herself from Mia's sleeping form, she slid out of bed as quietly as possible, her gaze darting around the room for her scattered clothes. Their heated encounter seemed like an absurd dream now; as if her body had been possessed by some other force, driven by lust and the need for human touch. And though she couldn't deny that it had been incredible, the guilt and regret were quickly becoming too much to bear.

"Riley?" Mia murmured groggily, her eyes fluttering open as she caught sight of Riley hurriedly dressing. "What's wrong?"

"Nothing," Riley lied, brushing away the loose strands of blonde hair that clung to her damp forehead. "I just... I have to go."

"Are you sure? We could talk, or –" Mia glanced at the empty whiskey bottle on the floor "– maybe get some coffee?"

"Thanks, but I really can't. I... I have office hours," Riley forced a smile, trying to hide the turmoil that roiled within her. "Last night was..." she hesitated, searching for the right words, "...amazing. Truly. But I have to get back to my life, and... well, let's just leave it at that."

"Alright," Mia sighed, disappointment creeping across her delicate features. "I understand. Just... take care of yourself, okay?"

"I will." Riley swallowed hard, knowing that she was leaving behind something unique and powerful, but also aware that embracing the unplanned had never been her strong suit. She needed order, stability, and this? This was anything but.

With one last glance at Mia, who looked both vulnerable and achingly beautiful in the morning light, Riley slipped out of the soft and inviting apartment and into the hard and bright world beyond. All of this had been a mistake, and she couldn't afford to live in the fantasy any longer. As she hurried down the sidewalk, her thoughts already started returning to the familiar confines of academia.

Riley couldn't help but wonder if she would ever truly be able to reconcile her desire for adventure with her need for control.

Chapter 2

Mia lay naked in her bed, the sheets tangled around her legs as she stared at the ceiling. The door clicked closed behind Riley as she left, with nothing but silence remaining in the small studio apartment. With the way she ran off, it was pretty obvious that Riley wasn't going to call. And Mia hadn't thought to ask Riley for her number either, so this was likely the last she'd ever see of the enchanting blonde professor. The worst part was that Mia really liked her too.

But wanting something and being able to have it are very different states of being.

Mia was a mess, and her body ached from the lumpy mattress. Her curly black hair was tangled and splayed across her sweat stained pillow, and her eyes felt almost haunted. The smell of sweat and booze clung to her body, unwelcome reminders of the bar she'd met Riley in the night before.

Sighing, Mia rolled onto her side and scanned the small space that was now her home. The apartment wasn't much to look at – peeling paint on the walls, a tiny kitchenette with appliances that seemed to be from another era, and a single window that offered a view of the run-down complex's parking lot. It wasn't the life she'd imagined for herself, but then again, neither was living in Parrish Mills.

"New beginnings," she muttered to herself, trying to ignore the nagging feeling that something was missing. "That's what this is."

She took a deep breath, inhaling the scent of stale cigarette smoke that stubbornly clung to the drab curtains she'd inherited from the previous tenant. It reminded her of her former life, of the darkness that had threatened to consume her. But it also represented a chance to start over, to find some semblance of normalcy amidst the chaos that had once been her reality.

"Come on, Mia," she whispered, willing herself to rise. Her bare feet touched the cold wooden floor, sending a shiver up her spine. She wrapped her arms around her torso, her fingers tracing the pattern of one of her tattoos. "You've got this."

Mia was determined to keep herself on track. Dwelling on this and spending the day moping were not going to help her feel better, and deep down she knew it. There was no point obsessing over what she could have done better, or what what mistakes she must have made.

She had enough *real* mistakes to do that over anyways.

Mia stepped into her apartment's tiny shower, letting the lukewarm water cascade over her inked skin. The intricate tattoos adorning most of her body whispered their protective magic against the lukewarm water of the cheap, battered shower cubicle. They snaked around her limbs, curving gracefully along her collarbone and down her spine.

Riley had asked her for the stories behind her tattoos, and Mia had managed to steer the conversation away deftly. Mia didn't feel like explaining that they didn't "mean" things so much as "were" things – that her tattoos were largely arcane sigils, each with a spell bound into her flesh.

That wasn't really a "first night you meet someone" conversation.

She closed her eyes as she lathered her body with soap, relishing in the simple pleasure of feeling clean and refreshed. The same obtrusive thoughts that seemed to surface every day swirled to the forefront of her mind, a mix of anticipation and anxiety for the day ahead, but she pushed them away, focusing on the here-and-now.

Drying herself off, she donned a skirt and simple tank top – an outfit that was both comfortable and fitting for the heat wave that seemed to be assaulting the Indiana September. It also allowed Mia access to her tattoos, and had become almost her unofficial uniform as of late. Maybe it was paranoia, but having her spells at hand made her feel significantly safer.

As she stood in front of the mirror, applying just the slightest touch of makeup around her dark brown eyes, she tried to drum up the courage to get moving.

"Okay," she muttered under her breath as she pulled on her boots. "Let's do this." Grabbing her messenger bag, Mia gave herself a once-over before stepping outside.

The bright morning sun greeted Mia as she stepped out the door and exited her apartment. Its blinding rays painted the world in brilliant hues, but also overwhelmed the senses. She squinted slightly, shielding her eyes as she began her walk to work.

Parrish Mills was the epitome of a midwestern college town. It was an oasis of green along the Wabash river, surrounded by miles and miles of flat cornfields. Well kept sidewalks were lined with lush trees, whose turning leaves danced in the breeze. The neighborhoods were filled with a mix of older, ornate Victorian homes from the town's founding and post-war ranches built during the mid-20th century boom. About twenty-five thousand people lived there, making it far too large to be considered a small town, but far too small for anyone to consider it a real city.

"Morning, Mia!" called out Mrs. Hendricks, a kindly elderly woman who lived across the street. Her wrinkled face broke into a warm smile as she waved from her porch, a steaming cup of coffee cradled in her hands.

"Good morning, Mrs. Hendricks!" Mia replied, offering a genuine smile in return. Mrs. Hendricks had started greeting her every morning within the first few days of her moving in. Mia wasn't even sure how she learned her name to begin with, the elderly woman just sort of... knew it already.

Mia on the other hand had figured out Mrs. Hendricks's name from what was written on her mailbox.

As she continued her stroll, Mia passed by a bustling bakery, the irresistible aroma of freshly baked bread and pastries wafting through the air. Children laughed and played in front yards, their carefree energy a stark contrast to her own troubled past.

"Hey, weirdo!" shouted a teenage boy from across the street, leaning against his bicycle with a cheeky grin. "You sacrificing things to the devil in that witch store?"

"Maybe," Mia responded playfully, rolling her eyes. "If you're lucky."

She couldn't help but feel a sense of gratitude for the mundanity of it all. Parrish Mills offered a chance at a stable life – something she desperately needed after the last year. But as much as she tried to embrace the quietness of the town, a part of her still didn't trust it. Mia hadn't really *had* stability before, and it almost made her skin itch. She'd ended up on the street at fifteen, and spent the eleven years after that fending for herself alone.

Well, not *alone*. She'd had Sarah. God Mia missed Sarah.

"Focus, Mia," she whispered to herself, echoing familiar words and shaking off darker thoughts. "One day at a time."

As she made her way to the historic downtown, Mia's determination to face the challenges of the new day began to grow stronger. She'd only lived here a few weeks, but the sights and sounds of Parrish Mills were becoming familiar. They seemed to be serving as a reminder of what she was trying so hard to achieve: a fresh start, far from the darkness that had once threatened to consume her. And with each step she took, she felt more and more ready to embrace whatever lay ahead.

Last night's regrets were fading to a fresh morning of hope.

Mia strode up to the delicate stained-glass door of Markov Books, the sun casting colorful reflections on the sidewalk. As she pushed it open, the tinkling of a bell announced her arrival. The scent of incense and old books filled her nostrils, providing a comforting familiarity.

"Morning, Mia," said Mike, the manager, without looking up from his newspaper. His tone was as bland as his khaki pants.

"Morning, Mike," Mia replied, rolling her eyes. She slipped behind the counter and grabbed a stack of books that needed to be put out. As she went to work stocking the shelves, she couldn't help but glance at the section dedicated to demonology and possession, memories of Sarah's fate weighing heavily on her conscience.

"Doing that dark, weird brooding thing where you stare into space again?" Mike asked, setting down his newspaper and peering at her over a pair of reading glasses.

"None of your business," Mia snapped, immediately regretting her harsh response. Mike barely reacted though, simply shrugging before going back to his paper.

"Fine by me," he said flatly, leaving Mia to sort through a box of crystals on the counter. The repetitive task of organizing the various stones by type and size felt almost calming. To place each thing in the place it was supposed to be, to give it order, felt stabilizing. Mia wanted stability, or at least part of her did.

Another part of her wanted to be tossed about like a lifeboat on the ocean, careening side to side as each wave struck it. To surrender to something dark and let it run through her veins.

"Mike, do you ever wonder what it's like to be possessed?" Mia asked without thinking.

"Can't say I have," Mike replied, yawning. "Sounds like something best left to horror movies."

"Right," Mia murmured, burying her face in the box of crystals. She thought about confiding in him about her past addiction, but something told her he wouldn't understand – or even care. Was it really worth trying to find a way to connect with a man who looked like he'd be most at home in a mattress store?

"Hey, watch the counter for a sec," Mike said, getting up from his chair. "I'm gonna step out for a coffee."

"Sure thing," Mia replied, watching him leave before turning her attention back to the crystals. As she worked, her thoughts drifted to Sarah, remembering her own screams as Sarah pulled the demon from her body. The guilt gnawed at her insides, but she knew there was nothing she could do to change what happened – instead just make sure she never let it happen again.

It had been eleven months since she'd seen Sarah, and Mia feared she'd never be able to face her again.

"No more demons, Mia," she whispered to herself, clutching an amethyst crystal tightly in her hand. "You're stronger than that now."

With a deep breath, she continued sorting the crystals, trying to lose herself in the simple, repetitive task. She was determined to create a new life for herself in Parrish Mills, free from her past mistakes and the darkness that had once threatened to swallow her whole.

The hours passed, and the day wore on. By mid-afternoon, the unmistakable scent of burning herbs filled the air, a cleansing ritual to rid the esoteric bookstore of any lingering negative energies that Mike insisted on doing. It felt vaguely appropriative, but he was her boss so there wasn't much she could do about it. Mia carefully placed the last book on the shelf, her fingers gingerly brushing against the elaborate cover design.

"Great job, Mia," Mike said, his voice a monotone drone that contrasted with the vibrant surroundings. "These new tarot decks need to be sorted next."

"Sure thing, Mike," she replied, forcing a smile as she picked up a few decks and began organizing them. One of the new decks had a familiar set of symbols on its box, most likely chosen because it looked good according to some marketer... but it was eerily close to one of the sigils used in a greater demonic summoning, reminding her of a whole world of regrets again. She felt a shiver run down her spine as memories tried to resurface that Mia couldn't afford to dwell on.

"Are you okay?" Mike asked, genuine concern creeping into his otherwise emotionless voice.

"Fine," Mia responded quickly, pushing back the dark thoughts and focusing on the task at hand. "Just a bit chilly in here."

"Old building, I guess," he shrugged, turning back to his paperwork.

As Mia continued sorting the decks, she couldn't help but feel overwhelmed by the quiet. The emptiness gnawed at her, like an itch she couldn't quite scratch, and she yearned for something – anything – to fill the void.

"Hey, Mike," she said, trying to strike up a conversation in an effort to distract herself. "What do you usually do for fun around here?"

"Fun?" he echoed, pausing in thought. "I don't know. Watch TV, I guess. Maybe read a book."

"Right," Mia sighed, feeling more disheartened than before. She didn't want to admit it, but she was getting desperate for friends. People were nice to her here, but she was still having problems connecting. The only person it seemed like she'd connected with in town was Riley. Last night had been amazing. *Riley* had been amazing. Mia usually didn't feel bad when a one night stand ran off the next day, but Riley was different. Hell, she'd actually *liked* talking to Riley at the bar before going back to the apartment. Just the *talking* was great.

Mia really hoped she was wrong and that Riley would call her.

"Have you tried joining any local clubs?" Mike offered after a moment, looking up from his paperwork. "There's a gardening club that meets on Thursdays, or maybe a yoga class? There's that new community center that just got announced, maybe they have some groups you might join."

"Thanks for the suggestions," she said, genuinely appreciative of his misguided advice. Mike was trying, and that counted for something. "I'll look into it," she lied.

"Great," he replied, returning to his work.

Mia took a deep breath, trying to shake off the loneliness and focus on the positives – her newfound freedom and the opportunity to redefine herself. This was her chance to build a new life, far removed from the darkness of her past, and she was determined to seize it with both hands.

"New beginnings," she whispered to herself. She was trying to turn that into a mantra at this point. As the sun dipped below the horizon outside, casting long shadows across the worn wooden floor, Mia knew that she had taken another step toward reclaiming control over her life and her destiny.

Her days at the esoteric bookstore continued to pass. Each one pleasant but repetitive. But Mia would still be Mia, no matter where she went – haunted by a past she wanted to forget and feeling deeply alone.

Chapter 3

Riley stood in the foyer of the large Victorian-style home she had bought with her ex-fiancé, Jake, and sighed. The late afternoon sunlight streamed through the stained-glass windows that decorated the edge of the room, casting a kaleidoscope of colors across the hardwood floor. The house was meant to be the place they'd start a family, but now it felt like a mausoleum for their dead relationship.

"Okay, let's do this," she muttered, trying to shake off the dark thoughts. She pulled open a moving box labeled "Living Room" and began to unpack its contents. As she placed each item on the shelves and tables, her mind wandered back to the man who was supposed to be here with her, filling this space with laughter and love. Instead, she was left with an empty echo of what could have been.

Riley missed the warmth of his arms around her, even though she knew she shouldn't. The memories of his charming smile and the way he smelled still haunted her thoughts, and she found herself checking over her shoulder as if he would suddenly appear behind her.

"Damn you, Jake," she whispered, blinking back tears while opening another box. The loneliness crept in, settling itself into the corners of the room like cobwebs.

The house itself was a stunning example of Victorian architecture, complete with ornate trimmings, high ceilings, and grand staircases. The exterior boasted intricate woodwork and expansive wrap-around porches that seemed to invite one to sit and enjoy a glass of whiskey while watching the sunset. It was a dream home, one that Riley and Jake had fallen in love with immediately.

Inside, however, the house bore the weight of its history. The wallpaper was peeling in places, revealing layers of patterns from years gone by. They'd gotten a deal on the house with how many repairs it needed, and the plan was to fix it up together. Well, there was no "together" anymore. It was just Riley now, in a huge eight bedroom house full of creepy sounds.

And in the month Riley had lived here, creepy was definitely an understatement.

Dusty chandeliers hung above, swaying slightly – as if moved by unseen hands. The wooden floorboards creaked underfoot, and the dimly lit hallways seemed to stretch on forever, filled with shadows that danced just out of sight. It felt like someone was watching her almost constantly. Just thinking about it made the looming feeling of dread grow in her stomach.

She shook her head, berating herself for being so easily spooked. After all, it was just an old house – one she would soon fill with her own memories and laughter.

But as she continued to unpack, the sense of unease lingered in the air like a thick fog, wrapping itself around her as tightly as Jake's embrace once had. The house held secrets within its walls, whispering them softly to Riley as she tried to make the space her own.

"Things will get better," Riley promised herself, placing another knick-knack on the shelf. "I'll make this house mine, and everything will be okay." But even as she spoke the words, she still couldn't shake the feeling that something unseen watched her from the shadows, waiting for the perfect moment to reveal itself.

As night descended, long shadows spread themselves across the walls. Riley's footsteps echoed through the empty rooms as she wandered down the dimly lit hallways, a glass of whiskey in hand to help her unwind after a long day. She tried to ignore the oppressive feeling that weighed on her, but it clung like a shroud, thick and suffocating.

"Get a grip, Riley," she muttered to herself, taking a sip of her drink. "It's just an old house."

But as she continued down the corridor, the strange noises began – soft whispers that seemed to emanate from the walls themselves, sending tingles down her spine. The lights flickered, sharpening eerie shadows on the wallpapered surfaces. The air felt charged with an electric energy, causing the hairs on the back of her neck to stand on end.

"Hello?" she called out, her voice wavering slightly. "Is someone there?"

There was no response, only the continued whispers and creaking floorboards beneath her feet. She took a deep breath, trying to steady her nerves, but the unease continued to grow within her, like ivy wrapping around her heart.

"Okay, so maybe this house is a little creepy," she admitted, gripping her whiskey glass tighter. "But I've faced worse things than a few weird noises." And yet, despite her attempts at bravado, the fear gnawed at her insides, relentless and unyielding.

As she stood there, the temperature in the hallway seemed to drop suddenly, leaving her shivering in the cold draft that swept past her. The lights flickered again, plunging her into darkness for a moment before returning with a weak, sickly glow.

"Come on," she whispered fiercely to herself. "You're stronger than this. Don't be a cliche. You can handle a few spooky sounds and lights."

Even as she spoke the words, the feeling that she was being watched kept getting stronger. Her heart raced in her chest as she finished her whiskey, hoping the warmth would calm her rising nerves.

"Tomorrow," she promised herself, "I'll look into this further. I'll figure out what's wrong with the electrical stuff or whatever, and everything will be fine." With determination fueling her, Riley retreated to her bedroom, firmly closing the door behind her.

But even in the supposed safety of her room, the sense of unease was still boiling in her stomach. And as she lay in bed, listening to the whispers and creaks that echoed throughout the night, she couldn't shake the feeling that whatever was happening here was only going to get worse. She eventually fell asleep, but it was a restless one, leaving her tossing and turning.

Her body roused her late in the night, and Riley climbed out of bed to walk to the nearby bathroom. A sense of dread built as she opened the door to the hallway, but she tried to shake it off. After relieving herself, she started to shuffle back to her bed when she heard what sounded like whispers behind her.

Riley turned around slowly, not really sure if she was awake or dreaming. At the end of the hallway, at the top of the stairs near the access to the attic, a young woman seemed to float in the air. Wearing a red dress with dark hair cut in a french bob straight out of the 1920s, she seemed to be almost as surprised as Riley was at that moment.

Riley opened her mouth to speak, but as she blinked the woman disappeared.

Stunned and only half awake, Riley slowly went back to her room and hid under the covers, unsure if she'd dreamt the apparition or not.

* * * * * * * *

The morning sun greeted Riley with a mocking cheerfulness as it streamed through the gaps in her curtains. She groggily rubbed her eyes, the weight of last night's eerie events still hanging heavy on her.

"Alright," she muttered, rolling over and tossing aside her blankets. "Time to get my life together."

Riley stood up, stretching her limbs, and headed towards the living room to continue unpacking. As she approached the boxes, she stopped dead in her tracks. The items she had spent hours unpacking the day before were now piled haphazardly back into the cardboard boxes. Some of the boxes appearing to be half-repacked, others completely sealed again.

"What the hell?" she breathed, staring at the chaos before her. She tried to piece together what could've caused this bizarre turn of events. "Okay, Riley, think. Did I have do this in my sleep? No, that's ridiculous." Her mind raced, searching for a logical explanation but coming up empty.

She knelt down and tore open one of the resealed boxes, revealing its contents: books, clothes, and other personal items. She reached for her favorite whiskey glass, only to discover it was missing.

"Seriously?" Riley groaned, frustration mounting. "I just found that thing yesterday!"

Riley opened another box, and it was just full of all of her spoons. Every single spoon in her home was here, along with some she didn't recognize.

"There has to be a rational explanation for this," she said to herself, her voice trembling slightly. "This has to be connected to last night's... strangeness." She shook her head, her frustration giving way to a revived uneasy feeling in the pit of her stomach.

"Right, so, let's try to find that damn glass and keep going," she muttered, rummaging through another box. But as she searched, more items seemed to vanish right under her nose. Her favorite scarf, a pair of earrings, even her toothbrush – all gone without a trace.

And in their place… spoons? Just more spoons.

"Okay, this is officially too weird," Riley murmured, her hands shaking as she attempted to process the bizarre occurrences. The feeling of being watched hit her head on again, as if invisible eyes were watching and studying her. The air around her seemed to hum with an unsettling energy, making her skin crawl.

"Whoever – or whatever – you are!" she called out to the unseen presence, "This isn't funny! Give me back my things!"

Silence echoed through the house in response, the unsettling atmosphere only growing stronger. Riley clenched her fists, her resolve hardening.

"Fine. You want to play games? I can play games too." Her voice was filled with anger, even as fear gnawed at the edges of her mind. "I will figure this out, and I will make you stop."

Riley was angry, but also desperately trying not to surrender to fear. Determined to get to the bottom of these strange occurrences, she decided to investigate every corner of the house.

"Alright, let's start with the basics," she muttered to herself, pulling out her phone to search for any history of unusual events in the area. As she scrolled through the results, her heart raced in anticipation. "Nothing? Really?" she sighed in frustration. "Ghosts aren't real, so there has to be some explanation."

She pocketed her phone and ventured down the hallway, each step accompanied by the creaking of floorboards beneath her feet. The lights flickered again, heightening her sense of isolation.

"God damn it, you're losing your mind," she whispered, trying to reassure herself. "It's just an old house making noise, that's all."

As she explored, she began to take note of any possible causes for the disturbances. A drafty window here, a loose floorboard there – but none of it could explain the repacking boxes or disappearing items.

Or the god damned *spoons*.

"Maybe it's an animal?" she pondered aloud as she opened closet doors and peered into dark corners. "A raccoon or a squirrel, perhaps? But how would they pack boxes?"

She shook her head, her frustration mounting. Her thoughts were interrupted as she heard a sudden thud from upstairs. Startled, she froze in place, her heart pounding in her chest.

"Okay, okay," she whispered, trying to calm her racing mind. "Maybe it's just something falling over. Let's go see." Her voice wavered slightly, betraying her terror.

With hesitant steps, Riley ascended the staircase, the creaking floorboards groaning beneath her weight. The lights above her flickered again, casting a ghostly pallor over her face as she reached the landing.

"Hello?" she called out, steeling herself for any response. "Is someone there?"

The silence that followed was deafening. As she stood alone in the dim light, she couldn't shake the feeling that this was more than just an old house settling or the antics of a wayward animal. Something inexplicable was happening here, and she couldn't ignore it any longer.

"Fine," she said to the empty air, her voice resolute. "You want my attention? You've got it. Let's see what you've got."

Riley cautiously opened the door to the master bedroom, her eyes scanning the shadows that clung to the antique furniture. A sudden gust of cold air caused her to shiver, wrapping her arms around herself in a futile attempt at warmth. Just a draft. It had to be.

"Draft or not, I'm getting to the bottom of this." She ventured further into the room, her footsteps muffled by the plush carpet beneath her feet. As she reached out to open the closet door, it slammed shut with a resounding bang, making her jump back in alarm.

"Okay, seriously?" Riley scowled, her frustration mounting. "Can we just cut the theatrics and talk like civilized beings? Or am I really just talking to myself here?"

The silence that followed was deafening, almost mocking her boldness. Despite her growing fear, Riley refused to back down. She took a deep breath, steadying herself as she once again approached the closet door.

"Look, I don't know what's going on here, but I'm not leaving until I figure it out. So you might as well show yourself, or whatever it is you do."

A soft creaking sound drew her attention to the window behind her, where the curtains fluttered as if caught in an unseen breeze. She watched as they parted, revealing a small, dusty mirror hanging on the wall. The glass seemed to shimmer, beckoning her closer.

"Is this what you want me to see?" Riley asked, her curiosity overriding her fear. She stepped towards the mirror, her blue eyes narrowed with determination.

As she gazed into the reflective surface, an unexplainable feeling of dread washed over her. It was as if something ancient and malevolent was lurking just beyond the edge of her vision, waiting for her to let her guard down. Riley swallowed hard, her throat suddenly dry. "You can't scare me that easily, you know," she whispered, more to herself than anything else.

"Alright, let's do this." Taking another deep breath, Riley reached out and touched the mirror, feeling an icy chill run down her spine. She steeled herself for whatever lay ahead, ready to confront the dark secrets hidden within the walls of her new home.

The moment Riley's trembling fingers made contact with the cold glass, the room seemed to fracture into a thousand pieces. Shadows twisted and danced on the walls like a nightmarish ballet, growing darker and more ferocious. A cacophony of voices, whispers, and screams filled the air, surrounding her with an unbearable din.

"Stop!" she shouted, her voice barely audible over the chaos. She staggered back from the mirror, her heart pounding wildly in her chest. "This isn't real. It can't be."

But things only just seemed to escalate. The temperature in the room plummeted, and Riley could see her breath forming icy clouds in front of her face. The chandelier in the hall began to sway violently, its crystals clattering together in a discordant symphony.

"Fine," Riley gritted her teeth, trying to steady her breathing. "You're not going to drive me out of my own home." With each step she took, the floorboards creaked ominously beneath her feet. Determination burned within her, and she refused to let fear control her any longer.

As she moved through the house, none of this was getting better. The air around her seemed to pulse with energy, and objects tremored on shelves as if they were alive. She opened doors only to find them slamming shut behind her, trapping her in a never-ending maze of terror.

"Enough!" she yelled, tears streaming down her face. "This is bullshit and I don't need to put up with it!"

Scraping together whatever resolve she could, she grabbed her purse and stormed out of the house. Riley was on the edge of breaking, but she didn't want to admit it. Whatever forces were at play were just too much for her. Riley knew there had to be someone or something that could help her understand what was happening.

Rain pelted down outside, drenching her within moments, but she didn't care. Riley wasn't a church going person, so she made her way to the one place she thought she might find answer – the witchy bookstore on Grover Street. Getting out of her car downtown, she did her best to ignore the cold. Her boots splashing through puddles with each step as she walked past the quaint shops that littered the neighborhood, moving with purpose. She'd passed this place dozens of times before, but never actually set foot inside. But she'd also never had to deal with a full fledged haunting either.

The bell above the door chimed as she entered, announcing her arrival.

"Can I help you?" a soft voice asked from behind a stack of books.

"Uh, yeah," Riley said hesitantly, her heart still pounding from the horrors she had just experienced. "I'm having some... issues with my house. Strange things are happening, and I don't know what to do."

The woman who spoke stepped out from behind the stack, and Riley was met with a familiar face.

"So, uh, you didn't call," Mia said, brushing a lock of curly hair out of her face.

Chapter 4

"Mia?" Riley asked.

"Riley." Mia replied, raising an eyebrow and allowing herself a teasing grin. "Fancy seeing you here. Because, again, *you didn't call.*"

"Uh, yeah, hi," Riley stammered, her cheeks flushing a deep shade of pink. The tension between them was palpable, a mix of awkwardness and lingering desire from their one-night stand. To Mia if felt like biting into a granny smith apple, sour and sweet all at once.

"Is there something you're looking for? A book on how to make a graceful exit, perhaps?" Mia quipped, unable to resist poking fun at their last encounter. Riley's blush intensified, and Mia couldn't help but feel a twisted sense of satisfaction. It had been a week since their one night stand, and this was the first sign that the woman was even alive she'd gotten since then.

Mia really liked Riley, and it really *had* hurt when she'd run out that morning.

"Actually, no. I didn't even realize you worked here," Riley said, seeming almost to shrink before Mia's eyes. "I'm… I'm sorry about that. I just got out of a long term thing, and I was impulsive that night. You're incredibly nice and beautiful, but I just wasn't ready and I–"

"Whoa, whoa, whoa," Mia said, holding her hands up. "Take a breath, Riley. If you're not here for me, why did you come in?"

Riley's blush deepened, and she looked away, tugging self-consciously at her jacket. The tailored lines of the garment accentuated her slender waist, drawing attention to the curve of her hips and the shapely length of her legs. It was a sight Mia was finding increasingly difficult to ignore. Never before had Mia found someone in a pantsuit attractive.

"I'm here because I need help," Riley answered quietly.

"Help?" Mia echoed, her curiosity piqued. While she was disappointed that Riley was here for something that wasn't her, it was clear that something was deeply wrong. Mia leaned against the bookshelf, crossing her arms over her chest as she studied Riley's face hoping to get a better read of the situation.

"Something strange is happening in my house," Riley confessed, avoiding Mia's gaze as she fidgeted with the cuff of her sleeve. "There are... noises at night, things moving on their own. I even found boxes that I'd unpacked and put away suddenly repacked again. And I saw someone, a woman."

"Sounds like you've got yourself a classic haunting," Mia said thoughtfully, her mind already racing with possibilities. She knew she shouldn't get involved. She knew she wasn't ready to put herself into this kind of situation. But Riley looked absolutely helpless, standing there in front of her. There was something about the quiet desperation in Riley's eyes that made her want to swoop in and save the day.

"Can you help me?" Riley asked hesitantly, finally meeting Mia's eyes. "I came here because I didn't know where to start and I hoped someone here would."

Mia took a moment to consider the implications, weighing the risks against the potential rewards. Mia had stuck to protective magic and and material things for the last eleven months, and while the magic that worked with the dead was different, it lay temptingly close to the demon work that had taken over her life. Mia knew she shouldn't get involved. It wasn't safe for her.

But Riley looked so scared.

"Tell me about what you've experienced," Mia said quietly.

Mia couldn't help but notice the flush creeping up Riley's cheeks as she described the haunting – the way her fingers toyed with the edge of her blazer, the slight stammer in her voice. It was almost heartbreaking to see this poised and sophisticated woman so scared, and Mia found herself battling the urge to reach out and hold and comfort Riley. Part of Mia desperately wanted to tell the her it would be alright whether it would be or not.

"I sound like a lunatic, I know. If someone told me all of this I'd be backing away slowly if not outright running away," Riley said with an awkward chuckle, clearly trying to downplay her unease. "I know it sounds crazy, but I don't know what else to think."

"Crazy? Not at all. I've seen things with my own eyes far worse than this," Mia replied, her voice reassuring. She took a step closer, hoping to dispel the tension and put Riley more at ease. "And maybe this is all harmless. Maybe your ghost just wants to help with the unpacking. Maybe it doesn't like the way you've arranged the furniture. Or maybe it's just got a thing for pretty professors in well-tailored suits."

"Believe me," Riley said, smiling just a bit, "if there were any ghosts offering to help with the endless boxes, I might be less inclined to evict them." Good, she was calming down. And it was nice to see her smile too.

"Evicting ghosts can be tricky business," Mia said, matter of fact. "Sometimes it can take just asking them to leave, while others hold on tight. It varies by the spirit, but I'm sure we can find a way to deal with them. I might be able to help you. After all, I've been told I can be quite... persuasive. It's just..."

Riley swallowed hard, her eyes wide as they searched Mia's face. For a moment, neither of them spoke – the only sound in the dimly lit bookstore was the steady drumming of rain against the windowpanes. Mia's heart raced as she watched Riley slowly regain her composure, the vulnerability giving way to determination once more. Mia knew they were playing a dangerous game. Getting involved was probably a mistake. This would be like walking a tight rope in more than one way.

"Please, Mia," Riley implored, her voice pleading with a hint of desperation. "I can't do this alone, and somehow the fates have led me back to you when I came looking for help."

Mia hesitated, biting her lower lip as she tried to look at this objectively. She was letting her feelings for this woman color her decisions and take risks she really shouldn't. The temptations that could come by touching this part of the supernatural world were dangerous for her. Her recklessness in moments like this had hurt someone she loved. But Riley needed help, and no one else was around to give it. If Mia didn't do this, who would?

"Alright," Mia relented, finally meeting Riley's gaze again. "I'll check it out. But we have to be careful, okay? I've been down this road before, and it's not something you want to take lightly."

"Thank you," Riley breathed, relief flooding her face as she reached out to touch Mia's hand, sending a shiver up her spine. "I promise, I'll follow your lead and do whatever you say."

"Good," Mia replied, trying to ignore the way her heart raced at Riley's touch. "We'll start by going through your house so I can get a baseline understanding of what's there. From there I'll be able to figure out what we're actually dealing with."

As they made their plans, Mia couldn't help but feel a mix of excitement and trepidation. On one hand, she was eager to delve into the unknown, to uncover the secrets hidden within Riley's home. On the other, she knew all too well the dangers that lurked in the shadows, waiting to ensnare those who ventured too close.

"Let's do this," Mia murmured, her resolve firming as she looked into Riley's determined eyes. Together, they would face the darkness, and whatever it might bring.

"Let's do this," Riley echoed, her voice filled with equal parts fear and courage. And as they set off into the unknown, Mia couldn't help but feel that she was walking a dangerous line. There were so many ways that this could go wrong.

But she'd been hiding from this sort of thing for a while, and maybe now was time for her to stop.

****

The sun dipped low in the sky as Mia and Riley approached the large Queen Anne home, which cast a long, sinister shadow across the overgrown lawn. Ivy crept up the brick gates like tendrils reaching out to ensnare them. It was a house that seemed to loom over its surroundings, imposing itself upon the neighborhood with an air of foreboding.

"Here we are," Riley said, her voice wavering slightly as they stood before the darkened windows. "It looks even creepier at night."

Mia could see Riley's fear etched across her features, but she also could see determination lurking beneath the surface. She found it quite endearing, this mix of vulnerability and resolve.

"Let's go inside, shall we?" Mia suggested, trying to sound more confident than she felt. Her heart thudded in her chest as she crossed the threshold, feeling as if she were stepping into another world entirely.

The moment she entered the house, Mia sensed something was off. The atmosphere was heavy, pressing down on her like a weighted blanket. She could feel an unearthly presence lingering just beyond her perception, something palpable yet elusive, hidden in the shadows.

"Did you feel that?" Mia whispered, her breath catching in her throat as she glanced around the dimly lit foyer. It was as if the very walls were watching them, waiting for the right moment to strike.

"Feel what?" Riley asked, her eyes darting nervously from one corner of the room to another.

"There's something here," Mia replied, unable to keep the tremor from her voice. "Something's watching us."

"Great," Riley muttered, her hands wringing together in a gesture that belied her casual tone. "Just what I wanted to hear. I really was hoping you were going to just tell me I was crazy."

Things were going wrong already, but she couldn't tell Riley. The first rule when dealing with ghosts was to not let yourself get afraid. But panic was creeping into Mia faster than she expected. Something here felt just similar enough to her old life, and she couldn't let herself slip. She had to stay strong. She had to protect Riley.

"Stay close to me," Mia instructed, her protective instincts kicking in. "And whatever you do, don't let your guard down."

"Trust me," Riley said. "The last thing I want is to be caught off guard again."

As they ventured out of the foyer and into the house, Mia's panic was joined by a thrill of excitement, sending even more adrenaline coursing through her veins. It was dangerous, yes, but there was something undeniably exhilarating about standing on the precipice of the unknown, ready to dive headlong into the abyss.

"Please, keep talking," Mia urged Riley, her breath quickening as she tried to focus on the sound of her voice rather than the unnerving silence that permeated the house. "Tell me more about what you've experienced here. Anything that might help us understand what we're dealing with."

Mia didn't *really* need Riley to re-explain the haunting. They'd gone over it at the shop several times. But it was easier to keep moving if Mia had something to focus on. She also didn't want to admit that she found comfort in the sound of Riley's voice.

"Okay," Riley began, her own voice shaking slightly as she recounted the strange occurrences that had plagued her since moving in. "It started with the noises – footsteps in the hallways, whispers in the night..."

As they moved from the living room into a parlor, Mia couldn't help but notice the way the shadows seemed to come alive, slithering and twisting around them like living creatures. The air grew colder, the oppressive atmosphere weighing heavily on her chest.

A rune on the back of her neck seemed to itch a bit.

Mia thought back to the first time she'd experienced something like this. It had to be nine years ago? She couldn't have been older than seventeen when she broke into that abandoned house with Sarah, looking for somewhere to stay for the night. The thing they found in there scared the hell out of them, and really solidified Mia's path into witchcraft... and her later descent into demonic addiction.

"Did you hear that?" Riley whispered, her blue eyes wide with terror as a faint creak echoed through the hallway.

"Probably just the floorboards settling," Mia lied, trying to sound more confident than she felt. In truth, she knew all too well what was causing the sounds – the ghosts were drawing closer, their ethereal footsteps audible only to those who dared to listen.

"Or maybe it's not," Riley muttered, her gaze darting around the dim room as if searching for an unseen enemy. "Whatever's stalking us, it seems to be everywhere."

"Stay calm," Mia advised, her heart thumping in her chest as she sensed the growing presence of the spirits within the walls. She needed to keep Riley safe, even if it meant risking her own sanity in the process.

As they ventured down the darkened hallway, an eerie gust of wind sent papers swirling through the air, making them both jump. The sound of footsteps seemed to follow them, echoing through the empty rooms like the ghostly remnants of a long-lost memory. A feeling of malice was building. Something dark was here, and Mia felt it like it was trying to tighten a fist around her heart. Whatever it was was approaching fast, and they needed to get out of the hallway before it saw them.

"Riley, quickly – in here!" Mia hissed, suddenly grabbing Riley's arm and pulling her into a nearby closet.

The door slammed shut behind them, plunging them into near-total darkness.

"Wha-what's happening?" Riley stammered, her breath hot against Mia's cheek as their bodies pressed together in the confined space.

"Shh," Mia urged, her voice barely audible above the pounding of her own heart. The footsteps had stopped just outside the closet, and she could feel the malevolent gaze of the entity upon them, as though they were being watched by a hungry unseen eyes.

"Stay as still and quiet as you can," she whispered, her body trembling with fear and something else – a desire that burned through her like wildfire. They were pressed together in the cramped space, and Mia could feel Riley's heart beating as hard as hers.

"Are we...are we going to be okay?" Riley asked, her voice quivering with barely-contained terror.

"Of course we are," Mia lied again, her resolve wavering as fear threatened to overtake her. The rune on the back of Mia's neck felt like it was on fire, as whatever dark spirit lurked outside the closet oozed with malevolence. Mia had never encountered a ghost this angry before.

"Promise me," Riley whispered, her voice shaking. "Promise me it will be okay and that we'll get through this."

"I promise," Mia murmured, doing her best to keep her feelings in check. They were trapped, and Mia wasn't sure she could get things under control to confront this thing if it didn't move on. It seemed like an eternity that the raging spirit lingered in the hall, but after a few minutes the presence seemed to fade.

"Okay," she breathed, gathering her courage as the footsteps began to fade into the distance. "Let's get out of here."

As they emerged from the closet, Mia knew that their ordeal was far from over.

"Alright," Mia said, her voice still unsteady. "We need a plan."

"Right," Riley agreed, her eyes scanning the dimly lit hallway as if searching for any sign of the spirits that haunted her home. "What do you suggest?"

"This haunting feels like more than one spirit. This is ghosts as in *plural*," Mia explained, trying to maintain an air of confidence she didn't really feel. "We need to figure out what kind of ghosts we're dealing with. Then, we can come up with the best approach to banish them."

"Sounds like a place to start," Riley said with a determined nod, her fear momentarily replaced by the steely resolve of a woman who refused to be driven from her own home.

"Now we have a lot of ground to cover, because this house is huge," Mia said. "It's seriously just you in here?"

"We… uh… I got a deal," Riley shrugged.

"I can see why," Mia replied. "Let's start with the basement and work our way up from there. Also, I'd rather get it over with before things escalate even more."

"Are ghosts more likely to gather in the basement?" Riley asked.

"No, but it offers fewer methods of escape," Mia said. "You always want an exit strategy, and if something happens down there, there's a chance we'll be trapped."

"Oh great," Riley replied, leading Mia down a narrow staircase that seemed to descend into darkness. The air around them grew colder with each step, and Mia felt the hairs on the back of her neck stand on end.

As they reached the bottom of the stairs, Mia noticed how the shadows seemed to dance on the walls, creating eerie, distorted shapes. She could see boxes stacked haphazardly along one wall, and old pieces of furniture covered in dusty sheets. The basement was a treasure trove of forgotten memories from the home's previous owners, and it felt heavy with the weight of the past.

"Over here," Riley said, pointing to a corner where a strange pile of objects had been arranged. The items were precariously balanced, and mixed within the items appeared to be several animal carcasses in various states of decay.

"Riley, did you put this here?" Mia asked, her heart pounding in her chest as she fought to keep her fear in check.

"Of course not," Riley replied, her face pale as she stared at the gruesome arrangement. "I only went down here once the first day I moved in, and this definitely wasn't here then."

As they stood there, staring at the chilling display, Mia couldn't shake the feeling that everything was *off* about it. There wasn't a *smell*. There should be a smell. Was what they were looking at even real? It felt like something malevolent was watching them, lurking in the shadows and waiting for the perfect moment to strike, laughing at their shock. Whatever was here needed to be dealt with, not just for Riley's sake, but for her own sanity as well. Mia just had serious doubts that she was up to the task.

And she was *sure* it wasn't a demon. It couldn't be. But something about the anger she kept sensing in the space reminder her of the rage of one, and it would be so simple to destroy something like this if she just took the power of a demon into herself. She'd be able to quickly dispatch it if she just gave over herself and let a demon be their dark savior.

It would be *so so easy…*

Mia shook her head, trying to refocus and get herself back in the game. This was not a helpful line of thought, and wouldn't lead anywhere good.

"Let's get to work," Mia said, forcing a smile to her lips as she tried to project an air of confidence. "What I want to do is try and reach out to one of them. See if there's something the spirits can tell us."

"Right," Riley agreed. Mia wasn't sure if Riley was really confident, or if she was just trying to match Mia. Of course, Mia's confidence was all false bravado right now, so that really didn't bode well.

Mia's hands trembled as she pulled several candles out of her messenger bag. As she lit them her tattoos glowed faintly in response. She could feel the spirits pressing against her defenses, hungry and insistent, eager to discover what she was doing.

"Stay close to me," Mia warned Riley, her voice strained with the effort of maintaining her self-control. "Whatever you do, don't stray from my side."

Riley nodded. "I'm right here, Mia. I won't leave you."

The words provided a small measure of comfort, but Mia couldn't shake the unsettling feeling that she was standing on a precipice, teetering between the safety of the living and the seductive pull of the otherworldly. The ghosts whispered in her ear, their icy breath raising the hairs on the back of her neck, reminding her of the intoxicating power she had once wielded when possessed by demons.

"Are you okay?" Riley asked, her brow furrowed with concern as she watched Mia struggle to maintain her composure.

"Everything's fine," Mia lied, forcing a smile onto her face even as her heart raced with anxiety. "It's just...these spirits are strong, and they're trying to break through my barriers."

"Can you keep them out?"

"I hope so." She didn't want to admit it, but Mia knew that her control was slipping. Despite the sigils inked into her skin and the protective circle she had drawn around them, the ghosts' presence was growing stronger, more insistent, and she felt her resolve crumbling under the weight of their spectral advances.

"Maybe we should leave," Riley suggested, her voice barely above a whisper. "We can come back later, with reinforcements or something."

Mia hesitated, torn between her desire to help Riley and the overwhelming temptation of the supernatural world clawing at her sanity. She knew that if she stayed, she risked falling back into the clutches of demons and losing herself once more to that dark abyss.

"Maybe..." Mia conceded, her voice wavering with defeat. "I just...I don't know if I can do this."

"Hey, it's okay," Riley reassured her, placing a gentle hand on Mia's arm. "I don't want you to push yourself too hard. We can try another time."

Mia closed her eyes, taking a deep breath as she tried to steady her racing heart. She could sense the spirits watching them, waiting for an opportunity to strike, but she couldn't bring herself to face them, not when the cost might be her own soul.

"Let's go. I need to go," Mia whispered, her voice barely audible above the howling wind that had begun to whip through the basement. Together, they extinguished the candles and stepped out of the protective circle, leaving the darkness and the ghosts behind them as they made their way back up the stairs.

As they reached the safety of the living room, Mia couldn't help but feel like a coward, fleeing from the very thing she had sworn to fight. But the terror in her chest was a visceral reminder of the danger she faced. She didn't know if she had made the right choice – but she knew she needed to get out of this house.

"Thank you," Riley murmured, her expression filled with gratitude and understanding. "For trying."

"Y-yeah," Mia stammered, unable to meet Riley's gaze. "I'm sorry I couldn't do more."

"Hey," Riley said softly, lifting Mia's chin so that their eyes met. "You did plenty, and we'll find another way to deal with this. We can do this another time."

Mia shook her head, her throat tight with unshed tears. "No, I just... I just don't think I can help you."

As Mia left Riley's house, she couldn't help but feel a sense of loss as the door closed behind her. Whatever was here was so overwhelming it was overtaking Mia more and more by the second, and she just needed to get out.

Chapter 5

Mia's heart pounded in her chest as she sprinted away from Riley's house, the night air cold against her flushed cheeks. The scent of late blooming asters filled her nostrils, a cruel reminder of the innocence she had lost so long ago. She fumbled with her keys, her hands shaking as she unlocked her old, rusted truck and threw herself into the driver's seat.

"Get it together, Mia," she whispered to herself, gripping the steering wheel tightly. "You've got this under control." Her dark brown eyes darted to the protective sigils tattooed on her left arm, a wariness settling deep within her bones.

As her pickup roared to life, Mia glanced back at the warmly lit house she was leaving behind. Riley Whittaker, the woman who had reached out to her for help, seemed like a beacon of light – someone she could connect with. Someone who finally made her genuinely smile again. But the temptation was too much being around supernatural forces that strong again.

Mia couldn't help her. Mia could barely help herself.

The tires crunched on gravel as Mia sped away from Riley's house, her thoughts racing faster than her rusty pickup truck through the streets of Parrish Mills. She tried to focus on the comforting familiarity of the town's landmarks: the old water tower looming overhead, the graffiti-covered railroad bridge, the neon signs of small businesses flickering in the darkness. It all felt like a safe haven from the ghosts that haunted her past – but could it protect her from her personal demons threatening to resurface?

****

"Come on, Mia, this is going to be amazing," Sarah said, her eyes shining with excitement. Her chestnut brown hair cascaded down her back as she stood tall and strong, full of life and energy. There was no fear or hesitation in her expression – only anticipation for what was to come.

Sarah was always confident. Most people thought she was cold, but Mia knew the truth. Mia knew Sarah was the warmest, brightest star in the sky. The two stood in a derelict warehouse not far from the harbor. It belonged to some shipping company currently going through bankruptcy. All of the stock had been seized by the government, so it just sat empty, windowless, and a perfect, private place for Mia and Sarah to do what they wanted.

"I'm having second thoughts, Sarah," Mia replied, nervously glancing at the single tattoo on her forearm, a spell bound into a rune to help her channel magic. "We've never tried anything this powerful before, and I'm just not sure if I can handle it."

"This was your idea Mia," Sarah reassured her, gripping Mia's hand tightly. "Don't doubt yourself. I never do. Just think about how good this is going to feel."

"Really good," Mia smiled, wrapping her arms around Sarah. "And then I'll use it to make you feel good too."

"I'm looking forward to it," Sarah smiled. Sarah pushed a lock of Mia's curls out of her face and tucked it behind her ear. The warmth of Sarah's body against hers in the cold warehouse made Mia smile involuntarily, and without thinking, she kissed her.

"There'll be time for more of that later – we don't want to miss the apex." Sarah pulled back with a smile and bounce in her step, grabbing a satchel of supplies off the ground.

With that, they began the ritual, chanting words in an ancient tongue that would summon the demon. Wisps of smoke and dark energy began to wrap around them and an intoxicating scent filled the air – one of power and desire, intermingling with the saltwater breeze that seeped in through the cracks in the warehouse walls.

"Ready?" Sarah asked clutching a leather bound book they'd found at an estate sale, her voice barely audible above the rushing wind that accompanied the demon's arrival. She looked into Mia's dark brown eyes, seeking confirmation.

"Ready," Mia whispered, her heart pounding inside her chest.

Sarah continued the ritual, saying words that seemed to echo in her bones. With that, the dark energy coalesced and began to flow into Mia's vulnerable form. As the demon entered Mia's body, a shiver ran up her spine, followed by a surge of pleasure that made her gasp. They had done this so many times, but it always felt like the first. The sensation was unlike anything she'd ever experienced, a tingling warmth that spread outwards from her core, filling her with an insatiable hunger for more.

Sarah, fully in control of the ritual, guided the demon's energy within Mia, heightening the pleasure and making their connection even more intimate. Bound together by the supernatural forces at play, they were like two celestial bodies locked in a gravitational dance.

"Sarah," Mia moaned, her voice breathy and desperate. "This one's so powerful... I can't describe it."

"Let yourself feel it, Mia," Sarah urged, her eyes locked on Mia's, raw emotion making them shine with an almost otherworldly light. "Find its vulnerability. Then the real fun begins."

But as the pleasure grew more intense, so did the sense of danger lurking just beneath the surface. The thrill of taming the demonic force was intoxicating, but both women knew that losing control was not an option.

The air grew heavy and suffocating, as if the very atmosphere itself was thickening – a slow, relentless pressure that seeped into their bones. Shadows seemed to slither across the warehouse walls, wrapping themselves around Mia and Sarah like serpents.

"Sarah," Mia whispered, her voice trembling. "Something's wrong."

"Focus, Mia," Sarah replied, her voice steady despite the creeping sense of dread. "If you keep your focus, we can control it."

Mia tried to cling to the pleasure, to let it anchor her against the swelling darkness, but it felt as though tendrils of smoke were slipping through her fingers, impossible to hold onto. The demon's power surged within her, overwhelming and uncontrollable, a torrential storm threatening to drown her. They had done this sort of thing dozens of times, but this was different. This was so much more powerful than anything Mia had imagined.

"Sarah, I can't!" Mia cried out, her body wracked with both ecstasy and terror. "It's too much!"

"Focus, Mia!" Sarah insisted, gripping her hand tightly. "You can do this!"

But Mia could feel herself losing ground, slipping further and further into the abyss. The demonic force consumed her, like fire devouring dry timber, leaving nothing but ash in its wake. The warehouse seemed to close in around her, the shadows leering hungrily at the edges of her vision.

"Sarah, help me!" Mia pleaded, tears streaming down her face as she realized just how precarious her situation had become. She felt like she was drowning, like a storm was threatening to pull her under.

"Stay with me, Mia!" Sarah shouted, desperation cracking her voice. "You have to –"

The sound of shattering glass cut through the air, and for a moment, everything seemed to freeze. A shard of moonlight sliced through the darkness, illuminating the two like a twisted tableau: two young witches, bound by something far more sinister than either of them could have ever imagined.

A voice like gravel dragged words through Mia's head. *YES LITTLE ONE, SURRENDER TO TH'XI'NIRAN. LET ME HAVE YOUR FRAGILE LIFE.*

"Please," Mia sobbed, her voice barely audible above the deafening roar of the demon inside her. "I don't want to lose myself."

"Shit. Hold on," Sarah whispered, her eyes filled with determination. "I'll get you out of this. I said I wouldn't let anything happen to you and I meant it."

The air crackled with electricity, the warehouse now a battleground between love and darkness. Sarah's eyes locked onto Mia's, her voice unwavering as she spoke the ancient words that would free her love from the demon's grip.

"No'crai Am'urtus Th'xi'niran quai," she chanted, her hands tracing glowing symbols in the air. "Ga'rai Incti Th'xi'niran quai."

Each word seemed to cut through the oppressive atmosphere like a knife, weakening the demon's hold on Mia. But the ritual demanded more than just words – it demanded a sacrifice. And amidst the chaos, Sarah's love for Mia shone brighter than any fear could ever hope to extinguish.

"Take this, you bastard!" Sarah screamed into the void. She grabbed her pocket knife and sliced open her hand. "Th'kra Th'xi'niran quai."

Sarah pushed her bloody hand into the swarm of dark energy that was growing around Mia's shaking form. Searing pain roared through Mia's body, and she felt like her insides were on fire. Just as it felt like she was losing who she was, Sarah's hand grabbed her and began to tear her out of it.

"Hold on Mia!" Sarah yelled, as lifted the bloody pocket knife to the swirling maelstrom that threatened to swallow them both. "Suck a dick Th'xi'niran… GI'CH'RA TH'XI'NIRAN QUAI!"

Sarah's blood anchored into the demon. She began to rip it out of Mia, but it held hard. Pain seared through Mia's body as the demon tore away at her. Sarah poured her own energy through her palm on Mia's chest supplementing her power to keep her alive.

The demon clawed at Sarah too.

Sarah steeled herself, determined to save Mia. She pulled harder, wincing as she endured the searing pain of her soul being torn in two. She watched as a part of herself, a swirling mass of ethereal energy, was ripped from her body and pulled out by the strength of the demon. The agony was indescribable, but Sarah refused to succumb to it. This was her choice. Her sacrifice.

"Sarah... no..." Mia croaked out, the last vestiges of demonic control slipping away, replaced by horror at what her love had done.

"I love you, Mia," Sarah gasped, her strength waning. "I don't know what this will do to me, but if I can't say it again I need you to know that I love you."

"I love you too," Mia whispered, tears streaming down her face as the demon retreated, vanquished by Sarah's gift.

****

Mia fumbled with her keys as she struggled to open the door to her small studio apartment, her heart pounding as memories from that fateful night resurfaced. Pushing open the door, she felt as though the weight of her past bore down upon her like a truckload of bricks, making it difficult to breathe.

"Get a grip, Graves," she muttered to herself, shutting the door against the world outside. She leaned against it, her eyes closed as she tried to steady her breathing.

"Sarah," Mia whispered, her voice laced with guilt and sorrow. "I'm so sorry."

She could still feel the ghost of Sarah's love wrapped around her like a warm embrace, a reminder of the terrible price paid for her freedom. A price Sarah paid because Mia wanted them to take things further than they ever should have.

Mia knew she couldn't trust herself to see where the line was. She knew she couldn't trust herself to know when to stop. This Riley woman needed her help, but she just couldn't give it.

Mia peeled off her clothes and climbed into her bed. She slid beneath the cool sheets, seeking solace in their familiar embrace. The darkness seemed to seep into her soul, stealing away the last vestiges of warmth left by the memory of Sarah's touch.

"Riley," Mia whispered into the void, her voice barely audible even to herself. "Why do you have to be... you."

She pictured Riley's face, her eyes filled with fear as she pleaded for help. Mia wished she felt strong enough to help this woman. She wished she could be the confident witch she pretended to be. She wished she didn't feel so broken.

Mia just wished there was a way she could help.

Chapter 6

Riley stood outside Mia's apartment, her heart pounding and concern furrowing her brow. It had been two hours since Mia had bolted from her house, and Riley felt like she needed answers. She raised a hand to knock on the door, hesitating for just a moment before rapping her knuckles against the wood.

"Coming!" Mia's called from inside, her voice edged with anxiety.

Riley shifted her weight from foot to foot, her eyes darting around the dimly lit parking lot. It always amazed her how a place could look so ordinary on the outside, yet be filled with someone as extraordinary as Mia.

The door creaked open, revealing Mia wrapped in nothing but a blanket. It was pulled over her head like a hood, and she just looked so much smaller than Riley remembered. Her dark brown eyes were wide and bloodshot, and her long, curly black hair tangled around her face. She looked like she'd been through some kind of emotional hurricane, and Riley couldn't help but let out a small gasp at the sight.

"Riley," Mia said, her voice cracking. "What are you doing here?"

"Can I come in?" Riley asked cautiously, her blue eyes scanning Mia's face for any signs of resistance. "I was worried about you."

Mia hesitated and sighed, then nodded and stepped aside to let Riley in. The apartment was a chaotic mess, with books and clothes strewn about the floor, a contrast to how the small space had seemed the last time she was here. Riley felt the heat of embarrassment radiate off Mia, but she ignored it. There were more important things to focus on right now.

"Are you okay?" Riley asked gently, closing the door behind her. "What happened back there? You just... disappeared."

"Look, I..." Mia started, her eyes welling up with tears, "I'm not really in the mood to talk about it right now, alright?"

"Hey," Riley said softly, placing a hand on Mia's shoulder. "I just want to make sure you're okay, Mia. Whatever happened, we can figure it out."

Mia let out a shaky breath, her eyes darting from Riley to the floor and back again. She was visibly distressed, and it broke Riley's heart to see her like this. The mysterious, enigmatic witch she'd become entangled with was, in reality, just as vulnerable and scared as anyone else.

"Fine," Mia said finally, her voice barely audible. "Come sit down, and I'll try to explain."

Riley stepped further into the dimly lit apartment, a single lamp in the corner casting long shadows on the walls. She settled onto the worn-down couch, its cushions sinking beneath her weight, and watched as Mia wrapped the blanket tighter around herself and sat on the edge of her bed. There was a desperation in her eyes Riley hadn't seen before, and she couldn't help but feel a wave of empathy wash over her.

"Hey, it's okay," Riley murmured, reaching out to give Mia's hand a reassuring squeeze. "I'm here for you. Whatever you're going through, you're not alone right now."

Mia hesitated, her dark eyes seemed to be searching Riley's face for any hint of insincerity. But all that was there was genuine concern and unwavering support. A tear trickled down Mia's cheek, and she took a deep breath before speaking.

"Alright," she whispered, wiping away the tear with the back of her hand. "I don't really think I told you about my... addiction?"

"No, you didn't," Riley said slowly, wanting to be careful how she responded.

"I... I used to allow myself to be possessed... by demons... for, uh..." Mia managed to stammer out.

Riley blinked slowly, processing what Mia was trying to say. "Are you saying you were addicted to demonic possession? That's a thing?"

Mia nodded slowly. "It's... I feel so gross saying it out loud... but it's an intense experience. It feels so... I mean... I can't describe it. But it's dangerous."

"How dangerous?" Riley asked, leaning forward. "Like kill you dangerous?"

"Worse," Mia shook her head. "There are worse things than dying. Worse things that you can lose someone to than death."

Mia's words hung in the air for a moment, and Riley was unsure what to say.

"That's a lot," Riley said finally, breaking the silence. "I wish you would have told me. I don't know if I would have pushed you into helping me if you had."

"No, it's not your fault... I made that choice. And your house is likely just full of ghosts, not demons." Mia looked down at her hands, fidgeting with the frayed edges of the blanket. "And, I've been clean for a while now. It's been over eleven months since I last allowed a demon to possess me. But sometimes, like tonight... the craving is almost unbearable. The darkness of whatever's in your house just dragged it out of me."

"Is that why you disappeared?" Riley asked softly, her heart aching for Mia. "Because you were scared of relapsing?"

"Partially, yes," Mia admitted, her voice breaking. "But there's more to it than that. Tonight, when we were dealing with that ghost in your house... something happened. Something I don't fully understand yet, but it triggered something inside me. It made me want to run, to escape from whatever darkness is still lurking within me."

"Is there anything I can do to help?" Riley asked, her blue eyes filled with determination.

"Your showing up helps," Mia replied, her voice barely audible. "I know it's not much, but having someone who's willing to listen, who doesn't judge me or think I'm some kind of freak... it means a lot. I don't have a lot of friends these days."

"Of course," Riley promised, squeezing Mia's hand again. "I don't have a lot of people either."

As they sat there in the dim light of Mia's apartment, the weight of everything Mia said hung heavy between them. Mia wasn't anything like how Riley first imagined when they met in the bar a week before. Mia seemed to need her help as much as Riley needed hers.

"Listen, Mia," Riley said firmly, her blue eyes locked onto the witch's dark brown ones. "I can't go back to my house tonight. It's haunted, remember? So I'm staying here with you."

Mia hesitated for a moment, clearly torn between wanting to maintain her carefully constructed barriers and recognizing that she could use the company. "I don't know, there's not a lot of space here."

"Ghosts. In my house. You haven't gotten rid of them yet, and I have classes to teach," Riley insisted. "I can grade papers from my office on campus, but I can't sleep there. So I'm sleeping here."

Finally, Mia sighed and nodded, allowing herself a small, wry smile. "Fine. But don't think this means you get to boss me around in my own home, got it?"

"Wouldn't dream of it, although yes I'm probably going to do that anyway. This place is a mess," Riley replied, matching Mia's smirk as she settled more comfortably on the couch, secretly relieved that she'd have the chance to keep an eye on her new friend.

As they sat in the dimly lit room, the air heavy with the lingering scent of old cigarette smoke and dirty laundry, Riley's thoughts turned to the mundane issues of basic survival. "You hungry?" she asked, reaching for her phone. "I could order us some Chinese food."

"Sure," Mia agreed, looking almost grateful for the distraction. "Just no shrimp."

"Allergic?"

"No, I just hate shrimp," Mia replied.

"Got it. No shrimp... you lunatic," Riley confirmed with a smile, scrolling through the menu of the nearest takeout place on her phone. She glanced over at Mia, who was fidgeting with the edge of her blanket again, and felt a surge of protectiveness that surprised her. She wanted to learn more about this enigmatic woman, to help her through her struggles and fears. She'd put Mia on a pedestal, holding an idealized version of this woman in her head.

Now Mia was firmly on the ground, and Riley was finally seeing the real her.

"Hey, Mia?" Riley asked, trying to sound casual as she tapped the screen to place their order. "Once we've dealt with whatever's going on at my house, do you think we could... I don't know, hang out sometime? Like, as friends?"

Mia looked up at her, a mixture of surprise and vulnerability in her eyes. "You really want to be friends with me? Even after everything I've told you?"

"Of course," Riley replied, her voice warm and sincere. "I think we could both use a good friend right now. Turns out when my ex-fiancé left, all the people who I thought were *our* friends were really *his* friends. I know I definitely need new ones."

"Friends it is, then. But you didn't tell me you used to be engaged, and I *need* to hear about *that* now," Mia agreed, and as they waited for their food to arrive, the two women began to share stories and laughter, gradually weaving together the fragile strands of an unexpected bond.

After a bit, their delivery arrived with a simple knock at the door. Riley collected it, and the two women sat on the floor, clearing a space for their meal.

Over steaming containers of kung pao chicken and vegetable lo mein, Mia fiddled with her chopsticks, hesitating before revealing more about her past. Riley noticed the subtle tremble in Mia's hands and knew that whatever she was about to share wouldn't be easy.

"Riley, there's something else I need to tell you," Mia began, her voice wavering slightly. "I wasn't alone when I used to let myself get possessed. My ex was involved. Sarah."

"Sarah?" Riley asked gently, placing her own chopsticks down and giving Mia her full attention.

Mia took a shaky breath, her dark eyes filled with pain. "Sarah and I... we were close. We both struggled with addiction to demonic possession. I was the one who introduced her to it. I pushed her into more and more dangerous situations. And when things went bad... I couldn't save her."

As Mia spoke, a tear slipped down her cheek, leaving a glistening trail in its wake.

"Hey," Riley reached over to Mia, placing a comforting hand on Mia's trembling one. "I don't know what happened, but this Sarah loved you, right? I'm sure if she were still alive she wouldn't want you to feel responsible."

"Sarah's not dead," Mia said, looking up and holding back tears. "She's... I said there were things *worse* than dying, right?"

"Yes..." Riley said slowly.

"Sarah sacrificed a portion of her soul to save me," Mia said quietly. "It just... it made her someone else. And it's my fault." Mia paused, and looked up at the ceiling. "And the worst part? A part of me wishes I could do it again... to feel that rush again."

"That's... that's a lot," Riley said. "I can't imagine how hard that is to live with."

"Don't have any other choice," Mia said shaking her head. "That's why I'm so afraid to help you with your haunted house. I worry about what might happen if I get close to that kind of darkness again."

Riley squeezed Mia's hand reassuringly, feeling the pulse of connection strengthen with each shared moment. "Well you've got me now, and the only vices I'll indulge are my own... and they're demon-free," she promised with a small smile. "Might involve whiskey and a riding crop, but no demons."

Mia smiled through her tears, her expression both fragile and determined. "Out of all the random hookups with women I met in bars I've had, I'm not quite sure how I got lucky enough to have gone home with you, Riley," she whispered.

"Hookups? As in plural? So you do that a lot, huh," Riley replied with a soft chuckle. "Wait, you didn't even guess that I was the one knocking on your door. Who did you think you were opening the door for dressed in only a blanket?"

"I can't help it if I am enigmatic and mysterious," Mia joked, striking a dramatic pose. "And we all know that blood shot eyes and hair that looks like a tangled mess are what get all the girls' engines revving."

"Oh yes, you're just the image of sexiness, sitting on the floor in your underwear, wrapped in a blanket, with a piece of lo mein stuck to your chin," Riley laughed.

"I'm a trendsetter," Mia laughed. "I'm sure this look will be hitting the runway in Milan next season."

As they continued their meal, the weight seemed to lift off of Mia ever so slightly. Riley hadn't noticed how weighed down Mia had seemed before, and now she couldn't figure out how she'd missed it in the first place.

Mia's fingers absently traced the rim of her now-empty plate, her dark eyes clouded with a mix of trepidation and uncertainty. "Riley," she began hesitantly, her voice barely above a whisper. "I want to help you, I really do. But I can't ignore the risks that come with getting involved with the ghosts in your house."

The concern flooding Mia's face tugged at Riley's heartstrings, but she knew she had the feeling that running wasn't going to make things better. She reached out again, placing her hand over Mia's "I understand, Mia. And I don't want to push you into something you're not ready for."

"Thanks," Mia said softly, her gaze flickering between Riley's eyes and their clasped hands. "It's just... after everything I've been through, I can't help but worry about the potential consequences."

Riley squeezed Mia's hand gently, a determined gleam in her blue eyes as she leaned forward. "I know it's scary, but you said it's a ghost and not a demon. And if it's a demon, we'll skip all of this. I'll burn the house down and we'll collect the insurance."

Mia offered a small, grateful laugh, her grip on Riley's hand tightening ever so slightly. "Fake a gas leak, got it."

"Nah, it's an old house – we go for the wiring," Riley replied with a laugh.

"Oooh smart," Mia whispered, her eyes shimmering with unshed tears of gratitude. "Though once we get done with the ghosts, you might want to get that looked at anyways."

"Don't remind me," Riley said, her voice filled with confidence and sincerity. "Now pass the crab rangoon and we can start planning our next move. Together, we'll make sure the ghosts in my house don't stand a chance."

The two resumed eating, and their conversation flowing between laughter and shared fears. As the last remnants of their Chinese takeout lay forgotten on the floor, Riley and Mia sat side by side on the couch, the dim lighting of the room casting eerie shadows on their faces.

Riley thought the lighting was romantic when she first came here the night she met Mia, but now she realized it was because Mia just didn't own enough *lamps*.

"Alright," Mia said finally, turning to Riley with determination. "If we're going to do this, we need to be smart about it. I was overconfident today, stupidly thinking I could just feel out the place." Mia took a breath. "We'll start by gathering what we know, that's step one. Then step two is researching your house, its history, and any mysterious events that may have taken place there. After we do those two things, then we can start poking around directly."

"Sounds like a plan," Riley agreed, her heart swelling with gratitude at Mia's willingness to help. She couldn't remember the last time she'd felt such a strong connection with someone, and it was both comforting and terrifying.

"First things first," Mia continued, grabbing a notepad and pen from a nearby shelf. "Let's make a list of everything we know so far. Then, we can narrow down our search and focus on the most relevant information."

"Okay," Riley said thoughtfully, tapping her chin. "Well, there's the stuff you saw while we were there. Most of it's been like that – footsteps, whispers, and doors slamming shut on their own. And one time in the middle of the night, I thought I was dreaming at the time, but I'm pretty sure I saw a woman."

Mia scribbled down the details, nodding for Riley to continue. "A woman?"

"Right," Riley confirmed, shuddering at the memory of the spectral figure lurking in her hallway. "A beautiful woman was standing in the hallway, dressed in I think 1920s fashion? Gorgeous red dress. I was half awake, and she disappeared in almost an instant."

"Any idea who it might be?" Mia asked, her brow furrowed in concentration.

"None whatsoever," Riley admitted, feeling a pang of frustration. "But maybe if we dig into the house's past, maybe we'll find some answers."

"Maybe," Mia echoed, her gaze distant and pensive. "But we should also be prepared for the possibility that we won't like what we find."

"Whatever it is," Riley said firmly, meeting Mia's eyes with resolve, "I'd rather face it head-on than keep living in fear. Besides, I've got you, a bad ass, on my side now, right? "

Mia smiled, her expression equal parts grateful and protective. "Right. The streaked makeup gremlin sitting in her underwear wrapped in a blanket. Total bad ass."

"Absolutely," Riley replied with a smirk. "No idea how I'm resisting your allure."

"Alright," Mia declared, snapping the notepad shut and standing up with purpose. "We've got our starting point. Tomorrow, we'll hit the library and begin our research. Together, we'll get to the bottom of this ghostly mystery and banish those spirits from your home once and for all."

"Sounds like a plan," Riley agreed, feeling a renewed sense of determination coursing through her veins. "First thing. After I go teach class. And have office hours. And go to that Poli Sci department meeting if it isn't canceled. First thing after all of that."

"Busy lady," Mia smiled.

"For very little pay and without tenure," Riley nodded. "If that house wasn't full of ghosts, I'd never be able to afford the mortgage."

"Yeah, I'm feeling better about my squalor," Mia laughed.

"Alright," Riley yawned, stretching her arms above her head. "I'm going to crash. Early morning, you know. Eighty freshmen are counting on me to talk about NGOs for an hour while they sit on their phones ignoring me since they're all taking the course for GE credits."

"Sure," Mia replied, rolling her eyes playfully. "Early morning. Just don't hog the blankets, Whittaker."

"Wouldn't dream of it, Graves," Riley quipped as she climbed into the bed, feeling the softness of the sheets against her skin. The scent of Mia's shampoo – a sweet combination of jasmine and sandalwood – surrounded her, an unexpectedly soothing aroma that made her feel even more at ease in Mia's presence.

"Goodnight," Mia murmured, snuggling under the blanket next to Riley. Her warm body pressed against Riley's own.

"Night," Riley whispered back. She listened to Mia's steady breathing. The last time she was in this bed, she was full of passion and regret. This time Riley realized she just felt *safe*. And between Jake and the ghosts, it might be the first time in years that she'd felt that at all.

Chapter 7

Mia found herself standing in a dusty attic, the air thick with the musty scent of aged wood and forgotten memories. The beams above her head groaned as if in protest against their eternal burden, casting spiderweb-laden shadows on the shifting walls. Her heart quickened as she took in her surroundings, the long-forgotten trinkets and discarded furniture that seemed to hold secrets just beyond her reach.

"Riley?" Mia called out, her voice bouncing off the unfamiliar walls like a lost echo. A deep longing welled up within her, a desire to not be alone right now. "Are you here?"

Silence was her only answer, as though the very air had swallowed her words whole.

As she ventured deeper into the strange attic, the walls seemed to shift and warp around her, as if the room itself were alive. A sense of disorientation gripped Mia, her dark brown eyes flicking back and forth in an attempt to find some semblance of stability.

"Alright, this isn't funny," she muttered, her fingers tracing the protective sigils inked into her skin as she tried to summon a sense of calm. "Just breathe, Mia."

Suddenly, the world around her flickered as if reality itself had been plunged into darkness. She reached out instinctively, her hands meeting cold, unyielding walls on either side of her. Panic seized her chest as her breaths turned ragged and shallow. She was trapped, confined within a space that seemed to close in tighter by the second.

"Help!" Mia screamed into the void, her voice cracking with desperation. "Someone, please!"

She clawed at the walls, her nails scraping against rough plaster, each frantic movement fueled by the suffocating fear that threatened to consume her. She desperately searched for the strength that had carried her through countless battles with ghosts and demons, but it seemed to have abandoned her in this dark prison.

"Riley, where are you?" Mia whispered, her voice barely audible as she fought to control her mounting panic. "I can't do this alone."

In that moment of sheer terror, a single, desperate thought echoed through her mind: escape. Escape from the darkness, from the quiet, and from the crushing weight of isolation. If only she could find a way out, she knew she would be able to face whatever lay beyond these walls. She just needed to find the strength within herself to break free.

"Shh, my dear," a sweet, seductive voice whispered in Mia's ear, somehow slicing through the darkness and her harrowing fear. "You must calm down."

Mia felt soft hands on her hips, the unexpected touch causing her to jump. The gentle press of a woman's body against her back sent shivers down her spine. Her heart raced as she struggled to comprehend what was happening. Was this another trick of the darkness, or something more?

"Who are you?" Mia demanded, her voice quivering with uncertainty.

"Someone who can help, if you'll let me," the mysterious woman murmured, her breath warm on Mia's neck.

As Mia's breathing steadied, a sudden realization washed over her: she was dreaming. This nightmarish landscape couldn't harm her; it was just a figment of her subconscious. With that knowledge came a sense of relief, and she allowed herself to relax into the woman's delicate touch.

"Are you here to guide me out of this darkness?" Mia asked, her thoughts racing with possibilities.

"Perhaps," the woman replied coyly, her fingers tracing along Mia's tattoos, eliciting a shiver of pleasure from their intimate dance. "Or perhaps I'm here to show you something else entirely."

"Like what?" Mia inquired, curiosity and desire intertwining within her as she leaned into the woman's embrace.

"Things hidden deep within your soul, my dear," the woman whispered, her voice like silk. "Passions you have yet to explore, or maybe just someone interested in drawing your attention."

Mia's mind swirled with images of darkened rooms and forbidden encounters, her pulse quickening at the thought. The woman's tender touch seemed to ignite a fire within her, stoking a hunger that Mia didn't want to deny. It was both thrilling and terrifying, a dance with danger that Mia knew she should resist.

"Isn't it strange, though?" Mia mused, her thoughts weaving a tangled web. "Why would my mind create this dream, when I know the dangers of giving in to temptation?"

"Perhaps your subconscious desires are stronger than you realize," the woman suggested, her voice like honey as she continued to stroke Mia's skin, "And perhaps not all temptations should be treated equally. Perhaps there are some it's fine to give into. Touching darkness is not the same as surrendering yourself to it."

Mia found herself lost in the woman's words, the seductive cadence drawing her further and further in. She couldn't help but wonder if the mysterious figure was right–could this be a sign that she needed to embrace her darkness? Or was it just her longing for connection?

"Maybe," Mia whispered, her voice barely audible above the steady rhythm of her own breathing. "But how can I be sure?"

"Ah, my dear," the woman sighed, a mischievous smile playing on her lips as she leaned in closer. "That is a question only you can answer."

In the darkness, the woman's hands continued their exploration, tracing the intricate web of sigils that adorned Mia's body. The warmth of her touch felt like a ghostly caress, each stroke sending shivers down Mia's spine. She allowed herself to be engulfed by the sensation, her mind swimming in a sea of pleasure and curiosity.

"Who are you?" Mia asked, her voice laced with both desire and apprehension.

"Does it matter?" the woman replied, her breath hot against Mia's ear. "Maybe I'm no one, merely a figment of your imagination. I have been alone for so long, seeking connection, just as you have."

Mia's heart raced at the woman's words, and she found it difficult to resist the allure of the unknown. The thought of connecting with someone, even a dream, sent a thrill coursing through her veins.

"Show me," Mia whispered, her breath shaky and uneven. "Show me this connection you seek."

"Very well," the woman murmured, her voice soft as silk. Her fingers glided lower, slipping between Mia's thighs, deftly finding the most sensitive part of her. At the same time, her lips pressed against Mia's neck, leaving a trail of searing kisses along her shoulder.

Mia gasped, the intensity of the woman's touch igniting a fire within her. It was unlike anything she had ever experienced before–ethereal and otherworldly, yet undeniably real. The dual sensations of the woman's fingers and lips sent waves of pleasure crashing through her, threatening to drown her beneath their unrelenting tide.

"Is this what you wanted?" the woman asked, her voice teasing and seductive. "To feel something so powerful and raw that it transcends the boundaries of reality?"

"Y-yes," Mia stammered, her body trembling with ecstasy. "I want to feel alive, to be consumed by passion and desire."

"Then let go," the woman urged, her fingers working harder, faster, driving Mia closer and closer to the brink of oblivion. "Surrender to the pleasure, and let it consume you."

Mia's thoughts raced, a chaotic whirlwind of fear, excitement, and longing. She knew she was playing with fire, tempting fate by indulging in such a forbidden fantasy. But the pull of the darkness was too strong, its siren song too sweet to resist.

"Please," Mia begged, her voice barely a whisper as the pleasure built to an unbearable crescendo. "Don't stop."

"Very well," the woman murmured, granting Mia's request as she continued her relentless assault on her senses. She could feel the electric tingle of the woman's lips against her neck, the soft whispers that danced in the air like ghostly breaths, and the relentless fingers that teased and tormented her until she was on the precipice of losing control. "Then let go."

The words hung heavy in the air, like an invocation, a command for Mia to surrender herself completely to the darkness that threatened to swallow her whole. And in that moment, as the pleasure reached its feverish peak, Mia gave in.

"Please," she whispered, her voice thin and desperate as she succumbed to the ecstasy coursing through her veins.

"If you insist."

As the tidal wave of bliss crashed over her, Mia felt herself being torn away from reality, the very fabric of her existence unraveling beneath the onslaught of her climax. And just when she thought she might shatter into a thousand pieces, she snapped back into awareness, her eyes flying open as she found herself in her bed, tangled in her sweat-soaked sheets wrapped around her and Riley snoring quietly beside her.

Wha–what just happened? Her heart raced in her chest, her breath coming in ragged gasps as she struggled to make sense of the surreal encounter. It was the most intense dream she'd had in years. Mia slumped back into the pillow and just stared at the ceiling for a while, and thought about the woman in the darkness some more.

Chapter 8

Mia pushed open the door to Markov Books, stepping into a whirlwind of scents and colors. The air was heavy with the mingling aromas of incense, old books, and the ever-present tang of desperation that accompanied some of the cheap tat on display. She inhaled deeply, letting the familiar atmosphere envelop her like a cloak.

The store was an odd mix of the genuinely mystical and the utterly mundane. One moment, Mia would find herself gazing at delicately crafted silver pentacles and obscure grimoires filled with forgotten knowledge, while the next, she'd be surrounded by mass produced Llewelyn paperbacks, stuffed unicorns, and crystals most often purchased by college students and bored housewives looking for a little magic in their lives.

As Mia made her way through the cluttered aisles, she couldn't help but feel a sense of belonging amidst the chaos. This place seemed to mirror her own life: a jumble of darkness and light, fear and hope, held together by the thinnest threads of belief.

"Ah, there you are," came a voice from the back office. Mia turned in surprise, her eyes widening as they fell upon the woman who had spoken.

Zelda Markov stood before her, as enigmatic as the very store she owned. A woman in her mid-60s, Zelda's white hair cascaded down her back like a silvery waterfall, framing a face lined with the wisdom of countless years. Though this was the first time Mia had met her in person, she recognized her immediately from the photo on the store's website.

"Zelda... I mean, Ms. Markov," Mia murmured, her voice hushed in awe. She had heard whispers about the mysterious owner of the esoteric bookstore – tales of arcane knowledge and cryptic advice – but to finally meet her face-to-face seemed almost surreal.

"Tell me, my dear," Zelda began, her voice rich and velvety, "what brings you into our humble shop on your day off?"

"Y-you know who I am?" Mia stammered, taken aback. It wasn't insane that Zelda knew who she was, but it was certainly shocking. As far she knew, Zelda hadn't been in the shop a single time since Mia had started working there.

"Of course, darling," Zelda replied, her smirk never leaving her lips. "No one works for me without my knowing everything about them. I've heard whispers of your past in Boston... but everyone deserves a second chance, don't they?"

"You know about that?" Mia swallowed hard, her mind racing with the implications of Zelda's words.

"Oh it wasn't hard to piece together dear," Zelda smiled. "We're not a large community, and people talk. Especially about the girl who spent the last year tattooing more spells into her skin than anyone I've ever heard of. You're a bit conspicuous – especially in skirts that short."

"Ah, I mean... if I can reach the tattoo with my fingers, it's easier to activate and..."

"Oh, I'm not judging you dear. If I still had legs like those I'd be showing them off too," Zelda laughed. "If you'd met me forty years ago, you'd be lucky to find me with any clothes on at all. I was just stating a fact, not rendering judgment. Now what brings you in today."

"I, um, I came to do some research," Mia finally managed to say. Zelda was nothing like what she expected. "I need guidance on spirit magic – there are ghosts haunting my friend Riley's home, and I've been doubting whether or not I can handle it. The way I used to deal with this sort of thing was… uh, unhealthy to say the least? I need a new tack."

Zelda's eyes gleamed with interest at the mention of spirits, and she leaned forward, her white hair tumbling around her shoulders.

"Ah, you're used to using a flame thrower to kill an ant, and you realize life requires more nuance. Especially when those flame throwers often backfire," she mused, tapping her chin thoughtfully. "But don't forget that the spirits that dwell in the shadows can be cruel and unforgiving. Ghosts are usually just the spirits of people, and people can be just as evil as the 'flame throwers' you're afraid of. Often worse."

Mia nodded thoughtfully.

"A spirit may not be able to threaten your soul the way your monsters can," Zelda said. "But some can be quite dangerous. I'm confident you can handle it, but keep your guard up."

Zelda was a stranger, but Mia still felt far more comfortable with the reassurance from the older witch. She needed to learn everything she could about spirit magic that she'd skipped over the years, and fast.

"Thank you," Mia breathed, her eyes shining with gratitude. "I'll do whatever it takes to protect us both."

"Good," Zelda replied, her enigmatic smile never faltering. "Remember, my dear, the spirits may be powerful, but so too is the witch who dares to face them."

"That's literally on a bumper sticker we sell here," Mia said, folding her arms.

"Who do you think made the bumper sticker," Zelda said, winking at Mia. "It's a good seller. Something I can sell to the 'daughters of the witches you couldn't burn' crowd without feeling gross at the end of the day."

"They do help keep the store in business," Mia shrugged.

"Yes, but it's ahistoric nonsense, drives me mad. Co-opting a narrative of real victims as a tool of supposed empowerment by those who hold more in common with the oppressors than those they claim to venerate is a disgusting thing to do. Sorry," Zelda said shaking her head. "Your friend's house. That's what we're talking about. If I were you I'd be looking into the history of the home. Discover exactly who you're dealing with."

Mia nodded, her dark brown eyes filled with determination. "Actually, I already planned on going to the library later today with Riley once she finishes work, before that I'm going to the historical society. Maybe I'll find something there."

"Excellent ideas," Zelda agreed. "But don't forget the public records office as well. Sometimes the most vital information is hidden away in dusty old documents that few care to read."

"Thank you, Zelda. I admit I didn't think of that," Mia replied, grateful for the advice.

Zelda leaned closer, her voice low and cryptic, like wind rustling through long-forgotten ruins. "And remember, Mia, sometimes it's the whispers of the forgotten that hold more truth than any historical record. Seek out local legends, for they often contain kernels of truth buried beneath layers of myth."

"Where can I find these 'whispers?'" Mia asked, her curiosity piqued by Zelda's enigmatic words.

"Listen closely to the stories told by those who have lived here their entire lives – the elderly, the reclusive, the folks most people ignore. You may be surprised at what you learn," Zelda suggested. "I'd offer to help you out there, but honestly I've only been in this town twenty years or so. I'll admit my knowledge of local folklore is sometimes lacking."

Mia initially found herself nervous about asking locals about what they knew, but quickly remembered Mrs. Hendricks, her neighbor who made Zelda looked young. Mia was pretty sure she had lived in Parrish Mills since before time began.

"Thank you, Zelda," Mia said sincerely. "I'll follow your advice and see where it leads me."

"Good luck, my dear," Zelda replied, her knowing wink reminding Mia that the path she walked was as much a journey of self-discovery as it was a quest to protect those she cared for. "And remember, courage is the witch's weapon – wield it wisely."

"That is also one of the bumper stickers on the rack," Mia rolled her eyes.

"It's good though, right?" Zelda laughed. "My point is that first rule of dealing with ghosts is *controlling your fear*. It's easy for a spirit to harm the fearful, but the unafraid? Major pain in the ass for them. You probably already know that, but it seemed worth reiterating. Only the most dangerous spirits can harm you if there's no fear in your heart, and even then it takes all they can muster."

"It's easier to say 'don't be afraid' than it is to *actually* not be afraid," Mia sighed.

"True," Zelda nodded. "But you strike me as a woman more than capable of putting her fear aside when someone she cares about is in danger. I have faith in you."

"Well that makes one of us," Mia said, smirking.

"My dear, you have more magic etched into your flesh than most witches will ever touch in their entire lives. You have more tools at your disposal than I ever have," Zelda's lips curled into a mysterious smile, as if she were privy to some arcane secret. "Are those modified versions of Ranithan's firestarter sigils on your forearms? Do those… work?"

Mia nodded quietly. "Not exactly helpful in this particular situation, but yeah?"

"The girl who can literally throw fireballs is worried her witchcraft isn't strong enough," Zelda laughed to herself. "You know, Mia, you are a walking contradiction. So much self doubt bundled into someone who's transformed her body into a walking grimoire."

"Having access to power doesn't mean having access to the *right* power," Mia sighed.

"True, but sometimes the answers we seek are buried within us," Zelda said thoughtfully. "You strike me as a dreamer. Dreams can be powerful, revealing truths that might otherwise remain hidden."

Mia furrowed her brow. Her dreams usually brought her back to her days in Boston, and the nightmares bound into her memories. They were far from helpful.

"Sleep in the house," Zelda continued, her eyes gleaming with a mischievous glint. "Let your dreams guide you toward the truth."

"Are you suggesting I put myself in danger?" Mia asked, her voice wavering slightly.

"Quite the contrary, my dear," Zelda replied, her tone soothing. "Remember, if you're not scared of them, they will have have a hell of a time hurting you." She placed a hand on Mia's arm, her touch surprisingly warm and comforting.

With a determined nod, Mia looked into Zelda's eyes. "What you're suggesting sounds insane, but I'll give it a shot," she said, her voice steady and resolute.

"Ah, my dear, make sure you don't let your skepticism overwhelm you," Zelda replied, her enigmatic smile transforming into a warm grin. She gave Mia a final wink that seemed to hold the weight of centuries of knowledge. "Embrace the present, Mia, for it is within your grasp to shape your destiny. Ooh, that's good. I should write that one down..."

Mia laughed. Zelda was a remarkable woman for sure, somehow both mysterious and ordinary at the same time. "Thank you, Zelda. I appreciate it."

"Of course dear, and if you're still looking for a book, Hodglinger's Grimoire has some fantastic spells for dealing with the dead. Just ignore the incredibly racist bits," Zelda said with a smile. "It's behind the counter next to the rose quartz. And there's always Iggatol's censored compendium if you're desperate."

Chapter 9

Mia Graves stood in the dim light of the library patiently waiting for Riley. She'd been here for the last several hours, after spending some time at the historical society and the public records office. As she adjusted the messenger bag hanging from her shoulder, feeling the weight of the historical documents she had obtained throughout the day, Mia's thoughts considered what Zelda had told her earlier about dreams. It's funny, Mia knew this stuff, but having someone else say them out loud reminded her of what should have been obvious.

"Hey, Mia," came a voice from behind her. Riley approached, moving quickly with determination. "Did you find anything interesting?"

"Interesting doesn't even begin to cover it," Mia replied. She led Riley to a quiet corner of the library, where they sat down at a small table surrounded by tall bookshelves.

"Alright, let's see what you've got." Riley's anxiousness was palpable. Mia opened her bag and pulled out the copies of the records.

"Here," Mia said, sliding the papers across the table. "I went through everything I could find today and made copies of everything they'd let me."

"Thank you, Mia," Riley said sincerely, her eyes scanning the pages. "You have no idea how much this means to me."

Mia watched Riley rub her hands together in anticipation. It was obvious Riley was desperate for answers. Answers would be good right now.

"Riley," Mia began quietly. "Remember, we're just starting here. We might not find the final answers in this stack."

"I know. Thank you," Riley said softly, her eyes meeting Mia's in a moment of genuine gratitude. "It helps knowing I'm not alone in this. I know that's sounds cheesy, but it's true."

Mia smiled, nodding in agreement.

"Let's start with these first few pages," Riley suggested. "We can work our way through everything else afterward."

"Sounds like a plan," Mia agreed, excitement coursing through her veins. The library's quiet corner seemed to be the perfect setting for their shared investigation – a place where secrets could be unearthed and the past could come back to haunt them.

Riley's fingers trembled slightly as she turned the stark white photocopied pages of the records, her eyes scanning each entry with a mix of fascination and dread. The dim library lights cast eerie shadows across the table, adding to the haunting atmosphere that enveloped them.

"Listen to this," Riley breathed, leaning closer to Mia. "In 1902, a family of four died in their sleep from carbon monoxide poisoning. And then, exactly a decade later, another family was found dead under similar circumstances..."

"Sounds like they should have checked the chimney," Mia said, shaking her head. "Let's put that in the maybe pile. A little suspicious, but easily explained by poor maintenance."

But as Riley continued flipping through the records, Mia's attention was suddenly captured by something else – an old photograph tucked between the pages.

"Wait," she whispered, reaching out to gently pry the photo from its hiding place. "Look at this."

Riley paused her reading to look at the image Mia held before her. It depicted a young woman with short black hair styled into a french bob, her sultry gaze captivating and enigmatic. She wore a slinky silk dress that clung to her slender frame, the fabric shimmering in the soft light. There was something undeniably alluring about her, a magnetic pull that seemed impossible to resist.

"Who is she?" Riley asked, her voice barely audible.

"Lila Rose," Mia replied, her own voice hushed in reverence. "According to the attached article, she lived in the house during the 1920s. Her beauty was legendary, and she was rumored to have had many lovers. "

As Riley took in the details of Lila's visage, a look of recognition flashed across her face. "I know I've never seen this woman before, but she looks incredibly familiar. Why do I know that face?" But before she could dwell further on the unsettling sensation, Mia spoke again, her tone somber.

"I don't know, but her story doesn't have a happy ending," she said softly. "Lila vanished without a trace one night weeks before her wedding, leaving behind a broken heart and unanswered questions."

Riley frowned, her eyes still locked on the photo. "How tragic," she murmured, unable to tear her gaze away from Lila's enigmatic smile. "But also... sounds familiar."

"Yeah, except I don't think she moved to Chicago like Jake did. Most people are convinced she was murdered,"

Mia continued, feeling a strange mixture of pity and intrigue. "You didn't murder Jake, did you?"

"Only wish I did," Riley replied.

"Lila Rose's disappearance is just one of many mysteries surrounding your house. We need to keep digging if we want to uncover the truth," Mia continued.

"Wait a minute," Riley whispered, her voice barely audible as she grabbed Mia's arm. "I know why she looks familiar. I've seen her before. She was... she was the woman I saw in my house."

Mia's eyes widened with surprise. "You're absolutely certain?"

"One hundred percent," Riley replied, her fingers tracing the outline of Lila's face in the photo. "It was late at night, and I thought I was dreaming, but... she was there. That same seductive smile, those piercing eyes. Similar dress even. It was her."

A shiver ran down Mia's spine as she considered the implications of this revelation. They had put a face to one of the things haunting Riley's house. But was Lila Rose the driving malevolence Mia had felt, or just another restless spirit trapped by it? She was certainly captivating, that Mia couldn't deny.

"Riley, we need to find out more about her," Mia said firmly, her dark brown eyes locked onto her friend's. "We can't let this go."

"Agreed," Riley responded, an expression of determination setting firm in her face. "But where do we start?"

"My neighbor Mrs. Hendricks is in her nineties. I think she said once that she's lived her whole life here, so maybe she's heard stories? I wanted to talk to her anyways," Mia said. "I know this would have all happened before her time, but that sort of tale gets passed down in a community like this."

"Then let's take what we have and see if Mrs. Hendricks knows anything more about Lila or even the other spirits ruining my life," Riley replied.

Gathering their findings, the two women left the quiet corner of the library, the heavy door creaking shut behind them. As they walked along the sidewalk, the sun dipped low in the sky, casting long shadows that danced and stretched like the ghosts of memories past.

"Are you scared?" Mia asked suddenly, her voice gentle and laced with concern. "About what we might discover?"

Riley hesitated for a moment, clearly processing her feelings. This was a lot, and Mia knew that this whole thing had to be weighing down on Riley heavily.

"Terrified," she admitted softly. "But I need to know, Mia. I can't live in that house without understanding who – or what – is sharing it with me."

Mia nodded, her own fears mirrored in Riley's blue eyes. "Then we'll face it together," she promised, her grip on their research materials tightening. "We'll uncover the truth about Lila Rose and whatever else lies hidden within your home."

****

The brisk autumn air nipped at Mia and Riley's cheeks as they strode from downtown Parrish Mills into Mia's neighborhood, a symphony of crunching leaves echoing beneath their feet. Mia couldn't help but shiver, the chill settling deep in her bones – or perhaps it was the anticipation of what lay ahead.

"Are you cold?" Riley asked with a bit of concern in her voice.

"Just a little," Mia admitted. "September weather is a pain. Eighty degrees at noon, sixty degrees at four. But I'll be fine. I could warm myself up with a simple spell, but I don't want to waste the energy." She glanced up at the old Victorian house looming before them, its once-grand facade marred by peeling paint and slightly cracked windows. Normally it seemed welcoming and warm, but something about their mission made it seem almost sinister.

"Or you could just wear more clothes, we're literally across the street from your apartment" Riley said with a smirk. "I guess we're here though." They both stood there for a moment, taking in the sight of Mrs. Hendricks's home.

"Let's see what she has to say," Mia said, determination flickering in her dark brown eyes as she took a step forward. Riley nodded, steeling herself as she followed Mia up the creaky steps to the front door. Ghosts were one thing, having to actually talk to your neighbors were something else entirely.

Before they could even knock, the door creaked open, revealing Mrs. Hendricks's wrinkled face, a warm smile splitting her thin lips. "Ah, come in, dears," she beckoned, her voice soft and inviting. "It's always nice to have some visitors."

"Thank you, Mrs. Hendricks," Mia replied, stepping inside and glancing around the dimly lit entrance. She looked at this house every day stepping out her front door, but never expected to go inside.

"Please, call me Eleanor," Mrs. Hendricks insisted as she shuffled deeper into her home. "I just made some tea, if you'd like some."

As they followed their elderly host, Mia glanced around the living room. The decor of the room was a mix of flower prints and lace, and every surface was filled with one kind of knick knack or another.

"Have a seat, dear," Mrs. Hendricks gestured to a plush but worn armchair, her eyes twinkling with an almost mischievous glint.

"Thank you, Eleanor," Riley responded, sinking into the chair and taking a moment to gather her thoughts. It almost seemed like the chair was trying to eat her, and Mia tried not to laugh.

"What brings you two lovely young ladies to my door," Mrs. Hendricks said, pouring cups of tea for Mia and Riley. "I don't get many visitors these days."

"Well Mrs. Hendricks... Eleanor," Mia started nervously. "My friend Riley here recently bought a house at the corner of Third and Romney. The large Queen Anne Victorian? The blue one?"

"Oh my, the Rose House," Eleanor nodded. "I know it well."

"Well, she's been having some... odd experiences there?" Mia said cautiously, not sure how much she should reveal. "I've heard some strange things about it, and since I know you said you've lived in Parrish Mills your whole life, you might have learned some of the history of the house over the years."

"Oh dear, I would say so. Everyone knows that house is haunted," Mrs. Hendricks nodded. "So many terrible things happened there. I'm surprised the real estate agent didn't tell you."

"My ex handled the purchase," Riley sighed. "I own the house, but he's the one who did all the negotiating."

"Why, I remember when I was a young girl," Mrs. Hendricks began, her voice softening as she delved back into her memories. "We used to dare each other to stand on the porch of the Rose House, testing our bravery. My brother Chester once got so scared he wet himself. I made it a whole hour, and no one in the neighborhood was brave enough to try to beat my time."

Mia couldn't help but smile at the image of a young Mrs. Hendricks, pigtails blowing in the wind as she stood defiantly before the house. She could imagine the mix of excitement and terror that must have coursed through her veins. Eleanor Hendricks was definitely Mia's kind of people.

"Of course, it was all in good fun," Mrs. Hendricks continued, her eyes misty with nostalgia. "But there were always whispers about a dark, vengeful spirit haunting that house."

"Vengeful spirit?" Riley asked, her brows furrowing with concern.

"Indeed," the older woman replied, her expression growing grim. "A malevolent ghost with a terrifying presence and a violent nature. My parent's friends would speak of it in hushed tones when they thought we'd gone to bed, afraid to tempt its wrath."

Mia shuddered, recalling the sinister presence she had felt in Riley's home. Confirmation that other people had sensed it was both reassuring and terrifying.

"Did anyone ever encounter the vengeful spirit?" Mia asked, her curiosity piqued despite her fear.

"Many claimed they did," Mrs. Hendricks said, her voice barely above a whisper. "Some say they saw a figure looming in the shadows, while others spoke of strange noises and objects moving on their own."

"Well that sounds familiar," Riley replied, her fingers tapping nervously on the armrest of her chair. "We've got a real poltergeist on our hands."

"Oh I don't know the fancy terms for that sort of thing," Mrs. Hendricks confirmed, giving Riley a knowing look. "But you just can't deny the sense of dread that seems to emanate from the Rose House. It's like the very walls are infused with fear. Some say that's what got poor Lila Rose. The house is named for her family, you know."

"Tell us about Lila Rose," Riley ventured, curiosity getting the better of her. She picked up the warm teacup, seeking comfort in its familiar heat.

"Ah, Lila," Mrs. Hendricks mused, her voice dropping to a conspiratorial whisper. "Such a tragic tale, that one. Her family moved there in 1910 or so. She grew up in that house. She was a beautiful young woman, the talk of the town, really. Men wanted her, women wanted to be her..."

"So she was pretty popular," Riley said. She took a cautious sip of her tea, the warm liquid doing little to soothe her growing unease.

"Oh absolutely," Mrs. Hendricks agreed, a knowing smile playing at the corners of her lips. "But Lila was more than just a pretty face. She was smart, resourceful, and fiercely independent."

"Sounds like she was fun," Mia murmured, feeling a strange kinship with the mysterious woman from the past.

"Her disappearance rocked the town," Eleanor went on, her eyes glistening with unshed tears. "One day she was there, the next... gone without a trace."

"Could it have been foul play?" Riley asked, her mind racing with possibilities.

"Maybe, or maybe she simply chose to vanish, leaving behind a legacy of intrigue and unanswered questions." Mrs. Hendricks conceded, taking a slow sip of her tea. "But the story most of us believed as kids was that a dark spirit in that house didn't want her to leave, so it made sure she never did."

"Did they find any evidence? Any clues?" Mia asked, her curiosity growing stronger.

"Nothing," Mrs. Hendricks replied, shaking her head. "She was simply gone, as if swallowed by the shadows themselves. Mind you, all of this happened before I was born, I just know what people said years later."

Mia's mind raced, conjuring vivid images of Lila dressed in her finest garb, her laughter echoing through the grand halls of The Rose House. She imagined Lila's dark eyes twinkling with mischief and secrets, and suddenly understood why the ghostly figure had left such an indelible impression on Riley's mind. Mia found herself increasingly drawn to the mysterious woman and the enigma surrounding her fate.

Mrs. Hendricks took a slow sip of her tea, the cup clinking gently against the saucer as she set it down. "The legends say that Lila's spirit still haunts the Rose House, seeking closure for her untimely fate. Some believe she's the the true vengeful spirit that terrorizes the home, but others think she's merely trapped, a prisoner of that dark menace."

The women sat and talked for several hours. Eventually, the sun dipped low, casting a golden glow through the lace curtains as shadows stretched and danced across the room. The once steaming cups of tea now sat cold and forgotten on the table, their contents unfinished as the conversation had consumed every ounce of attention.

"Eleanor, thank you so much for sharing your stories and insights with us," Riley said, her eyes still reflecting the spark of curiosity that had been ignited within her. "Your knowledge has been invaluable."

"Absolutely, it's been a pleasure," Mia added, secretly fingering the tattooed sigils on her forearm. "It was so kind of you to let us into your home."

Mrs. Hendricks smiled warmly at them both, her eyes crinkling at the corners. "Oh any time my dearies. It's always a pleasure to see you about in the neighborhood Mia. Seeing you every morning has brightened my days quite a bit."

"Come on, Mia," Riley said. "We have work to do."

Mia nodded, following Riley out of Mrs. Hendricks's house. As the door closed behind them, the chill of the autumn air nipped at their faces, bringing with it a renewed sense of purpose.

"Riley," Mia began, her voice barely above a whisper. "I know this is going to sound crazy, but I can't shake the feeling that Lila is reaching out to us. That she needs our help."

Riley looked over at her. "Either that or she's the one we're afraid of."

The autumn leaves crunched beneath their feet as they walked across the street to Mia's apartment building, ready to calculate their next steps.

Chapter 10

"The plan is to get in and get out," Mia said as she put her rusty Ford Ranger into gear. "We're not going there to fight anything or banish anything – just get you some clothes so you're not rotating between the same two suits anymore."

"Right," Riley nodded, buckling her seatbelt. "In and out."

"And remember, it's daylight. Nothing can hurt you in there as long as you're not scared," Mia said, pulling out into the street. "If you're not scared, there's nothing to be scared of."

The drive to Riley's house was filled with an uneasy silence, both women lost in their thoughts. As they pulled up to the ivy-covered Victorian, Mia felt a chill run down her spine despite the warm sunlight. This place had a dark history, and it was way too clear.

Don't be scared and you'll be fine Mia.

"Alright, I'll just run upstairs to grab a few things," Riley said, her eyes flickering with determination. "Make yourself at home in the living room. I won't be long."

"Sure thing," Mia replied, watching as Riley disappeared up the staircase. She hesitated for a moment before stepping into the living room, feeling as if she were intruding upon some secret world not meant for her. The last time she was in this house, she'd fled in a panic. And now she was just casually strolling in.

"Casual" wasn't scared. If you're not scared, you're safe.

She glanced around the dimly lit space. Most of Riley's possessions were still in boxes, stacked on various pieces of furniture which looked like they hadn't found their final places in the room. The entire house felt like it was in a state of transition, not yet knowing what it was supposed to be.

How appropriate.

Mia heaved a sigh and slumped onto Riley's couch, feeling the weight of exhaustion tugging at her eyelids. The last few nights spent sharing her bed with Riley had been anything but restful; As much as Mia was growing to like Riley, she snored and had a habit of randomly kicking in her sleep.

And it also reminded Mia of how much she missed Sarah's comforting presence in her bed.

"Maybe I'll just close my eyes for a second," she mused, sinking into the plush cushions. "Riley should be back down soon."

The world seemed to fade to black as sleep almost immediately claimed her. Mia found herself standing in a cramped, run-down apartment, with the Boston streets clearly visible out the window. The peeling wallpaper and grimy windows were foreign to her, but the scattered objects strewn about the room felt like pieces of her past — remnants of her life with Sarah.

"Where am I?" she whispered, her voice echoing through the desolate space. A tarnished silver locket lay open on a rickety coffee table, displaying a faded photograph of Mia and Sarah, arms entwined and faces flushed with happiness. "Why here?"

"Well, fuck. Look who the cat dragged in," a familiar voice called out from behind her, the sarcastic lilt sending shivers down Mia's spine. She turned around, searching for the source.

"Sarah? Is that you?" Mia's heart ached at the mere thought of seeing her again, but she couldn't shake the creeping sensation that something was off. This place wasn't right – this wasn't where they'd lived. But these things were their things. Whatever place her dream had constructed, it was full of items she knew too well.

"Of course it's me." Sarah stepped out from the shadows, wearing an amused smirk. "It's my fucking apartment. Why the hell are *you* here? Why is this dream the one that's happening?"

"God, you look so different..." Mia stared at the woman before her, unable to believe her eyes. Gone was the long chestnut hair that had always framed Sarah's face so perfectly; in its place was a shorter, rebellious cut with the sides shaved, accentuating her intense brown eyes. "Your hair…"

"Did that months ago," Sarah said quietly, picking up the locket from the table and examining it. "I thought it was time for a change. Lots of things change."

Mia couldn't help but laugh, shaking her head in disbelief. "It suits you," she admitted, the familiar warmth of Sarah's presence enveloping her like a comforting blanket. But even amid the happiness of seeing her again, guilt gnawed at the pit of her stomach.

"Speaking of changes," Sarah said, her gaze sweeping over Mia's body and lingering on the numerous protective sigils inked on her skin. "I see you finally went through with your 'magic tattoo plan.' I never thought you'd actually do it. One was already kind of ridiculous."

Mia glanced down at the tattoos, memories of pain and fear resurfacing as she traced the intricate patterns with her fingertips. "Yeah, well... things got rough after you left. I needed something to keep me safe."

"After I left. An interesting rewrite of history there isn't it?" Sarah crossed her arms, her voice taking on an edge of sarcasm. "I'm the one here still in Boston, while you ran off to god knows where. You abandoned me a year ago, and now everyone's telling me you disappeared from Massachusetts altogether a month ago."

"Sarah, please," Mia begged, tears prickling at the corners of her eyes as the weight of her guilt threatened to crush her. "I'm sorry. I miss you every day. I love you so much, and I wish I could've done more to help you."

"Wow." Sarah's eyebrows shot up in surprise, the sarcasm slipping away for a moment. "Real life Mia would never be this emotionally honest. She'd have run away by now, leaving me to pick up the pieces. God, why am I dreaming about you. Must have fallen asleep on the bus again."

"Excuse me," Mia whispered, her heart aching with the vulnerability of her confession. "This isn't your dream, it's mine."

"Nope, pretty sure I'm not the figment of someone's imagination," Sarah's eyes narrowed, studying Mia as if she were an intricate puzzle. "You're just a ghost of what I've lost."

"Sarah, don't–" Mia began, but it was too late. The dream shifted around Mia, the crumbling apartment fading away to be replaced by something far darker and more uncertain. Mia was now standing in a dimly lit bedroom. Soft moonlight filtered through the curtains, casting a pale glow over the room. This felt like Riley's house, but these weren't Riley's things.

In front of the mirror, stood Lila. Her dark hair in a perfect bob, and her red dress clung to her body, accentuating every curve. She was an ethereal vision of sensuality, and Mia couldn't help but be drawn to her.

"Hello?" Lila said softly, her voice low and sultry as she caught sight of Mia's reflection in the mirror. Her voice sounded so familiar, but Mia didn't know why. "What a beautiful creature you are in the light. Your body is like a painting, how delightful."

"What's going on?" Mia asked, her heart racing with a mix of confusion and desire as she stepped closer to Lila. "Is this another dream?"

"Perhaps," Lila replied cryptically, her eyes never leaving Mia's as she continued to get dressed. "But I don't know if I'm the dream or the dreamer." She paused, letting her fingers trail over her collarbone before looping a delicate gold chain around her neck. "Either way, does it really matter?"

Mia hesitated, torn between her curiosity and the undeniable pull she felt toward Lila. A part of her wanted answers, to understand why her dreams were filled with these visceral, haunting encounters. And yet, the desire coursing through her veins was just as powerful, making it nearly impossible to resist the allure of Lila's presence. Mia was certain she knew where she'd heard Lila's voice before.

"Maybe it doesn't matter," Mia admitted finally, her voice barely more than a whisper as she reached out and touched Lila's shoulder, fingers brushing against the soft, warm skin. "But I need to know... are you real?"

"Real enough for this moment," Lila murmured, leaning into Mia's touch as she turned to face her. The air between them seemed to crackle with electricity, their bodies drawn together like magnets. "And in the end, isn't that all that matters?"

As Mia gazed into Lila's eyes, searching for answers that might never come, she couldn't help but wonder if maybe there was some truth to Lila's words. Perhaps, in this strange, mysterious world of dreams and ghosts, reality was simply a matter of perception.

And as the shadows danced around them, weaving together a tapestry of moonlight and darkness, Mia allowed herself to become lost in the enigma that was Lila Rose. The faint scent of perfume filled the air as their eyes locked in a silent dance of desire. The soft glow of moonlight filtered through the thin curtains, casting an ethereal light across Lila's delicate features.

"Are you afraid?" Lila asked with a teasing smile, her voice low and quiet as she took a step closer to Mia.

"Of you?" Mia responded, her heart racing in her chest. She had been preparing herself for ghosts, but this was different – this was intimacy, something raw and vulnerable that went beyond anything she'd experienced lately. "Maybe a little."

"Good," Lila murmured, reaching up to brush a stray curl from Mia's face. "Fear can be... exhilarating. It can heighten sensation, almost intoxicate you. But you don't need to be afraid of me. You certainly weren't the other night."

Mia shivered at Lila's touch, feeling the heat of it even through the veil of her dream. She couldn't deny the allure of this enigmatic spirit, the way Lila seemed to call to some hidden part of her soul that longed for connection and passion.

"Show me," Mia whispered, giving in to the magnetic pull between them.

As they closed the distance, their lips meeting in a feverish kiss, Mia felt a surge of electricity pass between them. It was as if their very souls were intertwined, bound together by some invisible, unbreakable thread.

"See?" Lila breathed against Mia's lips, her fingers trailing down Mia's arm. "Exhilarating."

Unable to resist any longer, Mia reached for the straps of Lila's dress, her fingers trembling with anticipation as she began to undress the beautiful ghost before her. As she pulled the fabric away, revealing the pale, flawless skin beneath, Mia thought she could almost see the faintest shimmer of energy surrounding Lila's body.

But just as Mia moved to explore more of Lila's body, a dark shadow passed over the room, its presence so oppressive and menacing that even the air seemed to grow thick with dread. A cold chill crept down Mia's spine, her instincts screaming at her that danger was near.

"Wait," she breathed, pulling away from Lila and scanning the shadows for any sign of the threat she sensed. "Something's not right..."

"Don't move," Lila whispered, pressing a finger to Mia's lips as she pulled her close once more. "I don't want him to see you. I'll keep you safe."

As the darkness loomed closer, threatening to swallow them whole, Mia found herself torn between the desire to heed Lila's words and the overwhelming urge to flee. But in this world where the lines between reality and illusion were blurred beyond recognition, how could she know which choice was the right one? How could she trust anything – even herself?

"Embrace me and stay and I'll keep you safe from him," Lila repeated, her voice a seductive promise in the midst of the encroaching shadows. And with a shuddering breath, Mia closed her eyes and let herself be consumed by the darkness.

"NO!" Mia gasped, her eyes flying open as she jolted upright on the couch. The sudden shift from dream to reality left her disoriented, her heart pounding wildly as she frantically scanned the room for signs of danger. The simple surroundings of Riley's living room offered little comfort as she struggled to catch her breath, the vividness of the dream still haunting her every thought.

"God damn it," she muttered under her breath, gripping the edges of the cushions beneath her as if they were a lifeline. She could feel the lingering traces of desire from her encounter with Lila, even as the dread from the encroaching shadows gnawed at the edges of her mind. "Zelda said 'dream in the house,' great fucking plan Zelda… yikes."

Mia shook her head, trying to dispel the images that threatened to overwhelm her. She needed to focus, to remind herself that she was safe – for now, at least. Taking a deep, steadying breath, she allowed herself a moment to process the emotional impact of what she had just experienced.

"Damn," she whispered, running a trembling hand through her long, curly black hair. This dream had been like the one she'd had the other night. So real. So urgent. As if there was something important hidden within its depths, waiting to be discovered.

"Was that really Sarah?" she wondered aloud, remembering the sarcastic jabs and unexpected honesty of their conversation. The short hair, the shaved sides of Sarah's head – all so unfamiliar, and yet so intrinsically her. And Lila... Despite the undeniable attraction between them, Mia couldn't shake the feeling that there was more to their meeting than just a chance encounter in the realm of dreams. It all probably meant something, but damned if Mia could be sure of what.

"Ugh, I need to get my head on straight," she groaned, rubbing her temples as if that could somehow ease the confusion swirling within her mind.

Riley appeared in the doorway, her arms laden with personal items and a look of concern etched across her face. "Mia, are you alright? I heard you yell something from upstairs."

"Took some bad advice and got taken for a ride," Mia replied, her dark eyes still clouded with the remnants of her dream. She shifted on the couch, trying to shake off the lingering sensations and memories. "I had this... intense dream. It felt important, somehow."

Curiosity piqued, Riley set her belongings down and pulled up a chair, her blue eyes fixed on Mia's face as she listened intently. "Tell me about it."

"First, I was in this rundown apartment in Boston – I didn't recognize the actual place, but it was filled with my old stuff from when I lived with Sarah," Mia said, her voice growing softer as she recalled the vivid details. "Sarah was there, different, but still definitely her. We talked, and it felt so real." She hesitated for a moment before continuing, "But that's not the important part. Then, I met Lila Rose. Lila Rose appeared in my dream, and we shared an intimate moment. But just as things were heating up, a dark shadow passed over the room, and I woke up feeling... disoriented."

"Sounds like quite the dream," Riley acknowledged, her brow furrowed in thought. "But did it mean anything, or did you just have a weird nap?"

"I don't know for sure, but I think it meant something," Mia admitted, chewing on her bottom lip. "The connection to Sarah might be a coincidence, but the appearance of Lila... that felt real. Like I'm fairly certain that was the actual spirit of Lila Rose."

"Alright," Riley said, nodding slowly.

"Let's dig deeper into the history of this place, check the rest of the records. There has to be something we've missed," Mia suggested, her resolve flickering back to life like a flame rekindled. "And I think it's about time I went further into my spell books to find solutions."

As they prepared to leave, the sun cast long shadows across the room, like spectral fingers reaching out to grasp at the unraveling threads of the past. But Mia and Riley stood strong, their curiosity and determination propelling them forward into the unknown.

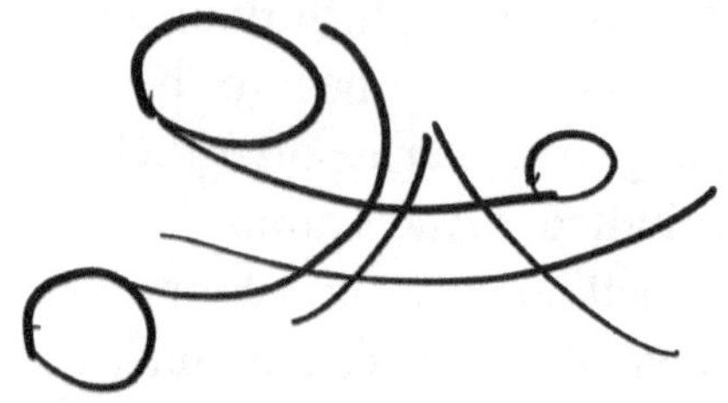

Chapter 11

Mia's fingers traced the faded words on a tattered page of a battered grimoire. Her apartment's single lamp was tilted over the desk and cast dark shadows across the small room. Her dark brown eyes scanned the intricate symbols and incantations as she muttered softly under her breath.

"Ah, there it is," she whispered, her voice tinged with excitement. She jotted down notes in her journal, sketches of the runes and sigils etched into her memory. The thrill of anticipation coursed through her veins, sending shivers down her spine. This was what she lived for – the unknown, the supernatural, the otherworldly. It made her feel alive, more so than anything else in her life ever had.

As Mia continued her research, the weight of her past struggles with addiction to demonic possession were still heavy in the air. She knew she had to be cautious, just one mistake could send her spiraling back into the darkness. But while magic had given birth to her darkness, it's also what pulled her out of it. Magical theory, and understanding the craft of a spell – that held more allure than anything else. She could embrace this part of it without worrying about slipping. This was the core of her witchcraft.

Outside Mia's window, the college town hummed with its usual late-night activity. But inside her sanctuary, she was immersed in a world of spirits and magic, preparing herself for the encounter that loomed ahead.

Across town, Riley sat hunched over her desk in her small office at Garrity University. The old newspapers and historical records Mia had gathered lay scattered around her, the musty smell of aged paper filling the air. With her long blonde hair pulled back into a messy ponytail, she squinted at the faded ink, piecing together the tragic history of her new home.

"1885... Mason Blackwood," she murmured to herself, her heart pounding with both trepidation and excitement. "Why did you do it, Mason? Why did you kill your family?" Riley took a sip of whiskey from a glass on her desk, savoring the warmth that spread through her chest. It was a small comfort amidst the chilling discoveries she was making.

Riley dug deeper and deeper into the history of the house. The articles she found about Mason Blackwood painted him as an absolute monster. If he was haunting the house, it was incredibly possible he was the "vengeful spirit" that plagued the house. Riley needed to know everything she could about him.

"Alright, Mason Blackwood," Riley whispered to the empty room, determination shining in her blue eyes. "Let's see if we can't figure out your secrets and put these spirits to rest."

Unbeknownst to them, as Mia and Riley delved deeper into their research, an unseen presence watched from afar, its malevolent gaze fixed on the two women who dared to challenge it.

****

Riley's footsteps echoed in the dimly lit parking lot as she approached Mia's apartment, her heart pounding with anticipation. The scent of incense wafted through the air, a comforting aroma that hinted at the witch's presence within. She reached for the knob, but before she had a chance to turn it, the door swung open to reveal Mia, looking equal parts exhausted and excited.

"Riley! I think I know what we should do next. I may have found what we need," Mia exclaimed, her eyes glittering with excitement. She ushered Riley inside, where piles of well worn spell books and grimoires were scattered across every surface.

"I think I did too," Riley replied, pulling out a folder filled with old newspaper clippings and historical records. "A man named Mason Blackwood built my house, and let's just say he had some serious family issues."

Mia raised an eyebrow, intrigued. "What kind of issues?" she asked, leaning against the kitchen counter.

"Mostly the kind where you end up killing them all with an axe," Riley said flatly, revealing the articles about Mason killing his family in 1885. "I think there's a good chance he might be the vengeful spirit we've been dealing with."

A tense silence fell over the room as the two women exchanged a knowing glance. Their determination to confront the ghost head-on only intensified, fueled by the chilling discoveries they'd made.

"Okay, that's big – but I've got some stuff on the practical front," Mia began, gesturing to the mess of notes scattered across her table, "I found a risky 'nuclear option' spell that could potentially deal with that thing. But if we fail..." Her voice trailed off as she looked down at her rune-covered arms. "If we fail, I'd risk cutting off my ability to do magic."

Riley shook her head, adamant. "That sounds a bit extreme, doesn't it? There's got to be another way."

"I mean, yeah – of course there is," Mia laughed. "Let a girl finish what she's saying. I'm saying that's our backup plan. The thing we do in case we fuck up everything else."

"Why did you start with the backup plan?" Riley sighed, putting her hand on her hip.

"You always start with the backup plan," Mia blinked. "If you don't, you never end up with one. Anyways, that's plan B."

"And plan A?" Riley asked.

"I've been brushing up on my spirit communication," Mia nodded. "It's possible there may be a way of talking our way out of this. Or punching."

"Punching?"

"Long story, the problem is that right now, the ghosts in the house can see us, but we can't see them. They can push us around, but we can't push back. It's hard to figure out how many of them there are or what they want right now," Mia explained. "So I figured that rather than starting with doing something to *them*... we'd do something *to ourselves* instead."

"What exactly did you have in mind?" Riley said cautiously.

"Something that would attune us to see the ghosts even when they want to be hidden," Mia answered. "You can't talk to what you can't see... so I'm going to fix that. So to answer your question, plan A is 'find out what they want.'"

"I can get onboard with that," Riley nodded.

"Great. The spell isn't all that difficult," Mia explained excitedly. "I'm also going to bind part of it into one of my tattoos... which should give it some extra oomph for me."

"Fantastic," Riley said, trying to quell her growing anxiety. "When should we do it?"

"Tonight," Mia sighed. "Then we need to test it at the house and see how well it worked. We can go to your house on a bright Saturday morning – just to play it safe."

"Deal," Riley said, feeling a mixture of relief and apprehension course through her veins.

Mia began to prepare the ritual, while Riley collapsed on the couch. This was going to be a long night.

****

Early Saturday morning, the sun's rays streamed through the windows of Riley's home, casting a deceptive sense of warmth and safety. But as Mia and Riley stepped inside, they couldn't ignore the ominous energy that seemed to cling to every corner. The presence of something dark and vengeful had intensified, casting an invisible shadow throughout the house.

"Did you hear that?" Riley whispered, her voice barely audible above the sound of her own pounding heart.

"The whispers? Yeah, I hear them too," Mia confirmed, her grip tightening around her bag of magical supplies. "Seems like our ghostly friends aren't too happy about our visit."

"Let him be unhappy. We're not backing down now," Riley declared, her blue eyes filled with resolve.

"I need you to be ready – things are going to be a lot more intense this time through," Mia said quietly. "You're going to see things that would be invisible to most people now."

As the two women made their way deeper into the haunted house, sounds reverberated around them. Doors seemed to open and close on their own, and shadows moved in the corners. Things that would have escaped their notice before now seemed amplified and filling the space.

Riley and Mia's footsteps echoed through the empty hallway, creating an eerie rhythm that only increased the malevolent atmosphere. Sweat beaded on Riley's forehead.

"Alright," Mia said, her voice steady despite the tension coiling around them. "Want to see a neat trick?"

Riley watched, fascinated, as Mia traced a finger along the intricate tattoo on her right collar bone. A surge of power rippled through the room, causing the air to crackle with electricity. Mia's eyes closed briefly, a low sigh escaping her lips as she reveled in the tingling sensation flooding her veins. When her dark brown eyes opened, they were alight with determination.

"Okay," Mia assured her, "I can physically interact with the spirits now."

"Hence the 'punching' remark the other night," Riley said laughing, her heart hammering wildly in her chest. "You certainly have a flare for the dramatic."

As they continued their exploration, Riley felt a cold dread seep into her bones. The ghosts were no longer just shadows lurking at the corners of her vision – they were suddenly all too real. Bodies seemed to push out of the walls. Their ghastly faces twisted in anguish, their spectral forms reaching out to touch her, to draw her into their world of misery and torment.

"Fuck off!" Riley screamed at one particularly persistent apparition. To her amazement, it vanished, dissolving into wisps of ethereal mist.

"Wow," she marveled, catching her breath. "That actually worked."

"Seems like you've discovered a new method of ghost repelling," Mia teased, a hint of humor shining through the darkness. "If you're angry, you're not scared. Keep it up."

"Fuck off!" Riley yelled again as another ghost materialized before her, its undead gaze locked onto her. Once more, the spirit disappeared.

"Ha! Take that, you creepy bastards!" she crowed before turning to Mia with a gleeful grin. "This is turning out to be a lot less scary than I thought it would."

"Careful," Mia warned, her tone laced with sarcasm. "You're a few whiskey shots away from becoming insufferable."

"Speaking of which," Riley mused, her thoughts veering towards the comforting embrace of amber liquid. "Whiskey might be a nice reward after this is all over."

"Deal," Mia agreed, her smile genuine for a fleeting moment before it was swallowed by the grim reality of their mission. "But, like, wait until after three P.M. to start."

"I mean, yeah. No shi–Fuck off!" Riley shouted once more at another encroaching ghost, her newfound confidence fueling her determination to reclaim her home. "Why is it this easy? I could have been doing this the whole time?"

"It makes sense if you think about it," Mia laughed. "Assholes never seem to be affected by ghosts like this, so the solution is to act like an asshole."

"Really should have let Jake have the house," Riley said with a quiet smirk. "He would have loved it here."

"There are a lot of ghosts here," Mia said. "Far more than you'd expect even in a house this old. We need to find one of the big ones."

The air grew colder, the haunting whispers of a dark presence intensifying as Mia and Riley ventured deeper into the home. Shadows danced along the walls, morphing into twisted shapes and grotesque faces that seemed to leer at them from every corner.

"Riley," Mia whispered, her voice shaking with a mixture of fear and adrenaline. "Right now we're a single target, if we're going to learn anything I think we're going to need to divide their attention."

"Damn," Riley muttered. "So split up?"

"Yeah, split up," Mia nodded, her dark eyes flickering with determination. "We need to cover more ground. I'll go upstairs, you head down. Maybe check the basement again."

"Are you sure?" Riley questioned, her blue eyes wide with uncertainty.

"Well no, but if we don't take some risks we probably won't learn anything," Mia replied, steeling herself for what lay ahead. "Stay safe, and remember what I taught you. And if you need to run for the door, do it. Don't hesitate."

"Right," Riley nodded, taking a deep breath. "See you on the other side."

As they separated, Mia felt the weight of the darkness pressing in on her. Her heart pounded in her chest, each beat echoing through the silence as she ascended the creaking stairs. She absentmindedly ran her fingers over the sigil on her collarbone as it resonated with low and steady power.

"Show yourself!" Mia demanded, her voice cracking the stillness like a whip. Something dark and spiteful responded with a sinister laugh that seemed to come from everywhere and nowhere at once.

"Leave this place," the spirit hissed, its malevolence palpable in the air. Mia refused to back down, her resolve unwavering.

"Give me one reason," she challenged, her dark eyes ablaze with defiance.

"Death will come for you," the spirit warned, its chilling presence engulfing Mia with an icy dread.

"If you wait long enough, that's true for everyone," Mia replied, her voice laced with sarcasm. "Please try and be more specific, would you?"

She could hear Riley's muffled shouts from downstairs, her friend taking on the ghosts that still lingered in the lower levels of the house. The thought of Riley yelling obscenities at the spirits filling the house drove her forward as she searched for the source of the vengeful spirit's power.

If you're angry, you're not afraid.

"Come on," she muttered under her breath, her fingers trembling as she felt the cold presence of the spirit drawing near. "You've got to give me something more than idle threats!"

The silence stretched out, heavy and oppressive, before the dark spirit finally made its move. A sudden gust of frigid air tore through the hallway, sending Mia staggering backwards into the wall.

"Is that all you've got?" Mia taunted, pushing herself off the wall and regaining her footing.

"I'm trying to warn you, he's asleep right now but soon he'll be awake," the spirit whispered menacingly, the temperature plummeting even further as Mia braced herself for whatever horrors awaited her upstairs.

She continued down the dark hallway, each step echoing through the dimly lit space like a death knell. "That's not a helpful answer," Mia said to the empty hall. "Just give me what I'm looking for."

"And what exactly *are* you searching for?" A velvety voice whispered into Mia's ear, so close she could practically feel the ghostly breath on her skin. She whirled around, coming face to face with Lila. The phantom beauty stood before her, draped in shadows, her eyes smoldering like dying embers.

"Well I'm not completely sure, but you are what I *wanted* to be looking for," Mia said, trying to keep her composure.

"Perhaps I'm what wanted to be found," Lila purred, taking a step closer, her spectral form flickering between solid and ethereal. "You seem keen on ignoring the other residents' warnings."

"Listen, Ms. Rose, I need to know what exactly is happening in this house," Mia was desperately hanging on to what little calm she could muster. The beautiful specter before her was both alluring and terrifying.

"Always so serious, aren't you, darling?" Lila teased. "But I must admit, there's something incredibly appealing about your determination."

"Stop playing games," Mia said, her heart pounding as she attempted to maintain her cool. "This is important."

"Very well," Lila sighed, disappointment tinging her words. "What do you need?"

"Is there a place that's safe for us to talk?" Mia said, her eyes darting around the dark hallway. "Somewhere that prying eyes and ears can't see us."

"The attic," Lila replied, her playful tone replaced with a solemn whisper. "I'm usually left alone up there."

Mia paused for a second. She was really going to do this. She was going to follow the ghost of a mysterious woman into the attic of a haunted house like it was nothing. *Well fuck, why not?*

Mia opened the door to the attic stairs, and ascended the creaking steps. As she entered the attic, it revealed a dusty, cobweb-filled space that felt eerily familiar. The atmosphere seemed to crackle with energy, heightening Mia's senses and making her painfully aware of Lila's presence beside her.

"Now that we're alone, what can I help you with?" Lila asked, her voice barely audible as she moved closer, her intoxicating scent filling Mia's nostrils. Their eyes locked, and the world around them seemed to fade away for Mia.

"I honestly don't know," Mia whispered, goosebumps forming on the back of her neck as Lila moved closer to her. "I'm going to admit, I didn't really have a plan beyond getting you talking."

"Really?" Lila breathed, her lips inches from Mia's. "And what do you think I might say?"

"I'm not sure, but hopefully something I could use to help my friend deal with the darkness in this home," Mia murmured, her heart thundering in her chest. Lila was so beautiful, and Mia was getting distracted by it.

"There is darkness here, but I'm not a part of it," Lila sighed, moving closer. Mia found herself feeling bold, and she quickly closed the distance between them, capturing Lila's lips in an gentle kiss that set their souls alight.

Lila pulled back after a moment in shock. "How is this possible, how are you touching me?"

Mia smiled and pointed at the sigil on her collarbone. "These aren't just for decoration. I'm a witch, it's a spell. That's kind of the beginning and end of it."

"This is... this is incredible," Lila said quietly, looking closely at the tattoo on Mia's collar bone. "Beyond dreams that always end so quickly, I haven't been touched by a living person since... since I passed." Lila hesitantly reached out, her fingers lightly brushing against Mia's skin.

"I can touch you more if you'd like," Mia leaned in and whispered to Lila. "You just have to ask."

Lila stood there for a moment quietly, considering Mia's offer.

"Please touch me?" Lila asked, breaking the silence. Her fingertips tenderly brushed against Mia's cheekbone, the sensation tingling with supernatural energy.

"I'd love to," Mia whispered, her heart beating even faster. She took Lila's hand and led her to an old chaise longue that must have been abandoned by a previous owner of the home, its fabric faded but still retaining a hint of elegance.

As they settled onto the chaise, Mia couldn't help but wonder if this was a mistake – if she was taking dangerous chances the way she did back in Boston. Was this just a needless risk that could endanger her life?

Mia didn't know, but she also knew she didn't care. She was finally feeling like herself again.

"Show me how it feels to be alive again," Lila murmured, her lips curling into a sly grin that made Mia's breath hitch.

Mia nodded, her hands delicately tracing the contours of Lila's body, her fingers gliding over the silk fabric of her dress. "I don't want to overwhelm you," she cautioned, her eyes searching Lila's for any sign of hesitation. "You need to tell me if it's too much."

"Never," Lila purred, leaning in to capture Mia's lips once more, their kiss deepening as their bodies pressed closer together.

Mia allowed herself to become lost in the moment, the taste of Lila's lips and the sensation of her ethereal touch igniting a fire within her like never before. As their passion intensified, the room seemed to come to life, the shadows dancing on the walls as though they were an audience to their otherworldly union.

"Your touch... it's incredible," Lila gasped, her voice breathy and filled with longing. "I never thought I'd feel this way again."

"Neither did I," Mia admitted, her voice thick with emotion as she continued to explore Lila's body, the mingling of the supernatural and sensual creating an experience that was both electrifying and intoxicating.

Mia moved her hands up Lila's dress, tracing the outline of her thighs and lifting the dress higher to expose her pale skin. She paused as her hand wandered up Lila's thigh, her fingertips pressing into the ethereal flesh.

"How have you endured this long without touch," Mia said, kissing Lila's neck.

"I don't know," Lila whispered, tilting her head back in ecstasy. "Please, don't stop."

"I won't," Mia promised, a tear rolling down her cheek. "Not until you ask me to."

Mia capturing Lila's lips once more in a passionate embrace as she continued to explore her body. Lila held onto Mia as hard as she could.

As Lila reached the peak of ecstasy, powerful energy surged through the air. The sigils on Mia's body glowed brighter, and flashes of light exploded throughout the attic.

"Did you feel that?" Lila asked breathlessly, her eyes wide with wonder.

"Yes," Mia breathed, her heart racing at the realization. "And I want to feel it again."

Lila smiled, and pushed Mia onto her back on the chaise. "I'll make you feel so much more."

****

With each shallow breath, the air in the attic grew denser, saturated with the scent of sweat and desire. The ethereal glow that previously enveloped Mia and Lila now gradually dissipated, leaving the two entwined on the chaise longue, their fingers lazily tracing patterns on each other's skin.

"Your sigils," Lila whispered, her fingertip hovering above one of Mia's glowing tattoos. "They're so beautiful."

Mia glanced down, marveling at the vivid colors that seemed to dance beneath the surface of her skin. "I never imagined they'd react like this," she murmured, her voice tinged with awe. "It's not how they're supposed to work."

"How do they work?" Lila agreed, a playful smile tugging at the corners of her lips. "Or at least how are they supposed to?"

"Different ones do different things?" Mia smiled. "Some are place holders... I can store different spells in them, and change what they do. Those are the weaker ones."

"What are the stronger ones?" Lila asked.

"Those are the permanent ones. I have to charge them from time to time, but they always do the same thing. Some are active, like the one I'm using to touch you," Mia gestured to her glowing right collarbone tattoo. "Some are passive, and always doing their work. Like, the ones on my chest and back, they're mostly protection spells. They do lots of things, like prevent anything from possessing me that I don't consent to."

"So you can only be taken by choice?" Lila said, looking at her. "Say, a dark spirit couldn't enter you and make you do something?"

"Not without my permission, no," Mia said, shaking her head.

"I wish... I wish I had something like that when I was alive," Lila said, her voice cracking.

"What happened to you Lila?" Mia asked quietly.

"I was going to leave... I was marrying Harold," Lila sighed. "We didn't love each other, but we were friends. He couldn't live the kind of life he wanted... love the kind of person he wanted. And my father was pressuring me to settle down, to quell the rumors."

"Rumors?" Mia asked.

"Well," Lila smiled. "I've been known to be quite free with my body."

"Ah," Mia smiled. "That."

"The marriage meant freedom, it meant leaving my father's house, leaving Parrish Mills," Lila continued. "My parents liked Harold, he came from a good family. Everything was going aces... and then, that night happened."

Mia just listened, stroking Lila's ethereal hair.

"I was getting ready to go out, have dinner and then spend time with some friends and go dancing. Harold and my cousin Janet would be there of course, so no one thought it was scandalous," Lila sighed. "As I finished getting ready, a shadow swept into my room. A man's voice told me that I wasn't allowed to leave. It said no daughter of his would ever leave.'"

"Your father?" Mia asked.

"No! My father was out east on a business trip!" Lila said, tearing up. "It was not my father's voice, it was someone or something else. It was something else. And then... then it forced itself into me."

Mia just held Lila firmly, letting the ghost explain.

"My body was out of my control, and I had to watch as it moved on its own, dragging me up into the attic," Lila choked through tears, and Mia's heart was breaking for her. "With my own hands, it made me seal myself in one of the walls. You asked me what happened to me... and the answer is right there."

Lila pointed to the north side of attic, to a wall that Mia only now realized probably wasn't supposed to be there.

"Oh god, Lila... that's terrible," Mia whispered.

"He doesn't come up to the attic much, which is why I usually stay up here," Lila sobbed. "It's why I stay away from the basement though. He likes the cold."

The basement. Where Riley was looking.

"Fuck," Mia leapt from the chaise like a cat, struggling to put her clothes back on as quickly as possible. She needed to get moving. She needed to get moving *now*. Lila looked at her with confusion.

"What's happening?" Lila asked, her voice shaking.

"Riley was going to the basement. I left her alone to go look down there," Mia answered, struggling to put her boots on. "With a homicidal ghost that can't keep track of who's who – and is apparently powerful enough to possess people."

"Go," Lila nodded. "Keep your friend safe. Get her out of the house. I'll be here if you can return."

"I hope I can come back," Mia said, kissing Lila on the forehead before running out of the room.

Mia crashed down the attic stairs, moving like a wrecking ball through the house, sending boxes flying as she barreled through any obstacle in her way.

"Riley!" Mia yelled at the top of her lungs, hoping for a response. "Riley, where the hell are you!"

Practically falling down the stairs, Mia slammed into the wall on the first floor landing. This wasn't about grace. This wasn't about agility. This was about brute forcing her way to get to Riley as fast as she could.

"Riley!" Mia screamed, her voice almost raw, running towards the basement stairs.

"Uh, yeah?"

Riley's voice had come from behind her. Mia tried to both turn around and stop simultaneously, causing her to lose her balance and violently crash into the floor, landing on her ass.

"Yikes, you beefed it there pretty bad Mia. You okay?" Riley asked, sitting on the living room sofa, eating a bag of chips.

"You're okay?" Mia asked, trying to catch her breath.

"Yes," Riley said, eating another chip.

"And you went into the basement?" Mia was exhausted and bruised now, and not in the fun way.

"Yesh?" Riley replied, her mouth full of half chewed Dorito.

"And there was nothing down there?" Mia asked, almost sounding desperate.

"I don't know, it was creepy as fuck," Riley replied. "I got Ben here to scope it out instead."

"Ben?" Mia asked.

Riley pointed across the room. Standing there was a boy, probably no more than twelve, dressed in old fashioned clothes. He was also translucent.

"What the shit, Riley?"

"He died in that 1902 carbon monoxide incident," Riley explained, eating another chip. "I told you that was a spooky thing."

"Hi Ben?" Mia asked, exasperated.

"Hello, Miss," the ghost answered.

"Did you find anything in the basement, Ben?" Mia asked. Why was she asking the ghost? Mia didn't know. But what the hell else was she going to do.

"Oh, the bad man is down there like usual, Miss. He's bad news," Ben nodded.

"Yeah, he told me that the moment I got down the basement stairs and I decided I'd rather just eat lunch and wait for you," Riley replied, crumpling up the now empty chip bag. "Also, I think we need to clean out my fridge. There are some leftovers in there that've gone bad."

"Riley, we need to leave right now," Mia said, the urgency in her voice clear and sharp.

"Is it because of Ben?" Riley asked. "Ben's great. His sister Gertie is around here too somewhere, she's adorable."

"Not because of Ben," Mia said, pulling herself back up to her feet. "Ben seems nice. Ben's fine. It's the 'bad man' I'm worried about."

"He's in the basement. It's fine," Riley sighed. "I think I'm getting okay with this supernatural stuff. Like, really acclimating. I feel like myself again, y'know? The ghosts are mostly just scared when you talk to them enough."

"The bad man can *leave* the basement, Riley. *He's the thing the ghosts are scared of,*" Mia walked over the couch, and started pulling Riley to her feet. "I met Lila Rose. The 'bad man' is the one who *killed* Lila Rose."

"Well that's not good, where is she?" Riley asked.

"Her body or her ghost?" Mia replied, walking the two of them to the front door.

"I mean, either I guess," Riley said, trying to not fall over as Mia pushed her out the door.

"The attic! *Both of them are in the attic, Riley*!" Mia yelled, as she stepped onto the porch, closing the door behind them.

Chapter 12

Mia and Riley returned to Mia's small apartment, and the door creaked shut behind them. Mia leaned against the back of the door for a moment, closing her eyes for a moment. She let out a deep breath before turning to Riley, who stood near the window, her blonde hair catching the light of the afternoon sun.

"Riley, there's something you need to know about the 'bad man' in the basement or whatever we're calling that thing," Mia began, her voice hushed as if the walls themselves might be listening. "It has the power to possess people, and when it does, the danger it poses is unimaginable."

Riley's eyes widened in horror as she processed the information. Mia continued, her voice steady but urgent, "That thing possessed Lila Rose back in the 1920s, and forced her to wall herself in up in the attic. That's why she's been stuck there all these years."

The words were like a steel weight sitting in the bottom of her stomach. Riley swallowed hard, and made a beeline to the small studio's kitchenette, where a bottle of whiskey sat on the counter. Grabbing a glass off the shelf, Riley poured herself a generous portion and took a deep breath.

Mia watched Riley carefully. She knew what she was saying might be difficult. She wished she had something more hopeful to tell Riley but there was no sugarcoating things when the stakes were this high.

Riley took a long sip from her glass, and turned to Mia. "It possesses people," Riley said slowly. "I know it's not a demon, but are you going to be okay around it? With your whole... thing?"

"I... uh... yeah?" Mia said. "I think so?"

"You'd tell me if you were getting in over your head, right?" Riley asked. "I don't want to be the reason you relapse."

"It's not a demon, it's a ghost," Mia replied. "I don't know until I know, and we need to get this done. If I find myself in over my head, I will tell you immediately. I promise."

Riley's eyes met Mia's, and for a moment, fear flickered across her face like a candle flame caught in a draft. But she nodded, the fire of determination returning to her gaze.

"Okay," Riley whispered, her voice resolute. "I trust you."

Riley's fingers tightened around her glass, clearly using the amber liquid as a security blanket. She took another swig, and leaned back against the counter clearly hiding a sense of fear and defeat.

"Riley, there's something else I need to tell you," Mia began hesitantly, her eyes flicking away from Riley's gaze. The vulnerability in her voice was audible, and Riley stepped forward, showing clear signs of concern.

"Alright, hit me," Riley said, clearly steeling herself for something awful.

"During our investigation at your house, Lila Rose and I... we had sex," Mia blurted out, her face flushed with a mixture of embarrassment and apprehension. She braced for Riley's reaction, expecting hurt or even betrayal.

Instead, Riley burst into laughter. A genuine, head-thrown-back, eye-watering roar of laughter. It was so unexpected that Mia couldn't help but stare in mild shock, her own lips twitching in response.

"Y-you're not upset?" Mia stammered, unable to hide her confusion.

"Upset?" Riley choked out between chuckles, wiping a stray tear from the corner of her eye. "Mia, you fucked a ghost. That's... that's just hilarious. Absurd and fucking hilarious."

Mia blinked, her mind reeling from the unexpected reaction. She'd anticipated jealousy or anger or even concern, but instead, found herself swept up in the infectious laughter that continued to bubble from Riley.

"Okay, okay," Riley managed to gasp, finally catching her breath. "I'm sorry, it's just... you literally *fucked a ghost*. That is, like... I didn't even think ghosts were real not too long ago, and now I'm crashing at the apartment of a one night stand who just *fucked a ghost* in my house."

"That is definitely one way to describe it," Mia admitted sheepishly, her cheeks still flushed as she allowed herself a small smile. "Lila has this magnetic pull, and things just... happened."

"Hey, no judgments here," Riley said, raising her glass in a mock salute. "You've got to explore the options in front of you, and apparently some of your options have been dead for a century."

As the laughter subsided, the Mia and Riley let their concerns float away for a moment. For right now they were just two friends laughing at a very weird thing that happened. The complexities of their lives seemed just a little bit more manageable, and the weight of the supernatural world seemed a bit lighter on their shoulders.

Mia glanced at the half-empty whiskey bottle on the counter, then back to Riley, who was still grinning from ear to ear. The dim light of the room cast shadows across her face, giving her a playful, almost mischievous expression.

"Okay, so maybe it's a little unconventional," Mia conceded, her voice tinged with amusement. "But can you really blame me? Lila is practically the embodiment of temptation, and she made it very clear that she wanted me."

Riley raised an eyebrow, swirling the amber liquid in her glass as she sat down on the worn couch cushions. "I'm not denying she's got a certain allure, but I think 'unconventional' might be an understatement, don't you?"

Mia couldn't help but smirk, feeling a mixture of relief and bemusement at Riley's casual acceptance of the situation. She poured herself her own drink and took a sip, allowing the warmth to spread through her chest as she considered her next words.

"Alright, I'll admit it's not exactly an everyday occurrence," she said, suddenly struck by a thought. "But if you'd been there, seen the way she moved, heard the tone of her voice... well, you might understand why I couldn't resist."

Riley chuckled, a deep, throaty laugh that seemed to resonate throughout the small apartment. "You know what, Mia? You're absolutely right. If I were in your shoes, I probably would have done the same thing. After all, how many chances do you get to fuck a ghost?"

"Exactly!" Mia exclaimed with a laugh. "And besides, it's not like you and I were pursuing a relationship." She paused, her eyes narrowing playfully. "Unless, of course, you're jealous?"

"Jealous?" Riley snorted, the corners of her mouth turning up into a lopsided smile. "I'm not proud of it, but if you remember I literally ran away after we slept together. I just got out of a long term relationship – I am so broken right now, I should not be dating *anyone*, let alone *you*."

"Good," Mia replied, her heart swelling with affection for her friend. "Because the last thing I need is a jealous roommate on top of everything else."

"If we get my house unhaunted, you won't have a roommate at all," Riley laughed, raising her glass.

As their laughter subsided, Riley sipped her whiskey thoughtfully, the amber liquid glinting in the dim light of Mia's apartment. "You know, once I stopped yelling 'fuck off' at every ghost I encountered in the house, most of them turned out to be pretty harmless – even kind," she admitted.

"Really?" Mia leaned forward, her curiosity piqued. Her dark eyes locked onto Riley's, searching for any hint of exaggeration.

"Believe it or not, they've been nothing but helpful after that initial... misunderstanding. Mostly I think they were worried about me," Riley continued. "There's a lady in a Victorian dress who showed me where the hidden compartments were in the pantry, and you met Ben. His little sister was running around before you came down too."

"Interesting," Mia mused, swirling her own drink. Her protective sigils seemed to gleam more brightly, as though responding to the conversation. "So it sounds like you're cool with all of the ghosts in your house except... y'know… that *other* one."

"Right," Riley agreed, her voice somber as she contemplated the malevolent entity that threatened her home. She took another sip of her whiskey, seeking solace in its warmth. "That thing needs to go. Not a fan of a murderous ghost in my house."

"Okay then," Mia said firmly, her gaze unwavering. "We'll deal with him, Riley. We won't let him ruin your life. The rest of them can stay."

"I think it's safe to assume we know what this 'thing' is," Riley said. "At this point I'm pretty certain it's the ghost of Mason Blackwood."

"Are we sure he's the ghost, or is it possible that it's whatever took control of him too? We are dealing with something that can possess people." Mia asked.

"I don't know, I can't be sure," Riley shrugged. "But digging into the history, I didn't find anything earlier."

"I mean, odds are good it *is* him," Mia said, shrugging. "But I also don't want to assign the wrong identity to it. Like, are we even sure it was a person to begin with?"

"What do you mean, why wouldn't it be a person?" Riley asked.

"Not all ghosts were once people," Mia explained. "Some are just... things."

"Well, let's go with something generic like 'vengeful spirit' for now, but it's probably Blackwood," Riley nodded. "Honestly, I don't know what I would do without you."

"Let's hope we never have to find out," Mia replied, her voice tinged with equal parts humor and sincerity. They clinked glasses, sealing their pact with a silent toast, and turned their attention to planning their next steps in the battle against the vengeful force that haunted Riley's home.

"So, I think I need time to formulate a proper plan," Mia said, her voice low and steady. "The vengeful spirit is our only mission now, and I need to find a banishing spell that won't burn me out. Right now I only have one I know that will work, but the risks are so high I need time to find an alternative. Talking with the ghosts was plan A, but this guy doesn't want to talk. And since plan B is the 'nuclear option,' I'd rather take the time to find a new plan A instead.."

"I don't even like considering this so called 'nuclear option,'" Riley asked hesitantly, her fingers tracing the rim of her whiskey glass as if seeking solace in its familiar curves. "So yeah, since we have the time, finding a new, better plan is for the best."

Mia sighed, the weight of responsibility settling heavily on her shoulders. "I hope there is one, Riley. But every other method I've researched so far has its own set of risks, and none are guaranteed to work against something as malevolent as this thing. But I'm not done, I have more books, and if all else fails I can look online."

"You gonna check witchtok?" Riley said with a wry smile.

"No I am not going to check 'witchtok,'" Mia laughed.

"What, you're saying that the people on TikTok aren't real witches?" Riley smirked.

"Oh no, plenty of them *are*, but no one's going to put something with real power on social media," Mia said shaking her head. "That's how you accidentally get a teenager blown up."

"Did not think about that," Riley said, looking thoughtful for a moment.

"Seriously though Riley, I have… I have real places I can look," Mia said. "I just need the prep time to Batman this."

Riley looked at Mia, her face becoming serious and her eyes filling with a mixture of fear and determination. "Then we'll take all the time you need," she declared. "As long as you're with me, I know we can do it."

"Thank you for trusting me, Riley," Mia replied.. "I won't let you down. We'll banish that murderous monster, and then you can learn to live alongside the other ghosts in your home, in peace."

Mia's dark brown eyes narrowed as she studied Riley's face, gauging her reaction to the grisly reality of what they were facing. The dim lighting of her studio apartment cast an eerie glow on their surroundings. She leaned forward, her long black curls falling around her face like a protective shroud as she spoke.

"Riley, I need you to promise me you'll stay away from the house until we've dealt with the vengeful spirit," Mia said firmly. "I can't emphasize enough how dangerous it is. We're not just talking about a prankster ghost here – we're dealing with something much more sinister."

Riley's fingers tightened around her glass, and she nodded solemnly. "I understand, Mia," she replied, her voice quivering slightly with apprehension. "I'll do whatever it takes to stay safe. I promise."

"Good," Mia said, her voice softening as her gaze locked onto Riley's. "Just remember that your safety is our top priority. No matter what happens, we need to put your well-being first."

Riley took a deep breath, her chest swelling with determination. "I promise, Mia. I'll prioritize my own safety, no matter what. And I trust you to do the same."

As they spoke, the air in the room seemed to thicken with reforming tension, the weight of what they needed to do felt like a bow string being pulled taught.

"Thank you, Riley," Mia whispered, her voice barely audible over the howling wind outside. "Just remember: we're in this together, and I'll do everything in my power to protect you."

Chapter 13

The air in Mia's studio apartment was still, like the quiet before a storm. The darkness of night seemed to press against the lone window as if seeking a way inside. The reflection of a street light cast a pale glow on the sleeping forms of Mia and Riley, their breathing slow and steady.

An icy gust of wind slipped through the cracks in the battered door frame, as an unseen malevolent presence wormed its way into the space. An angry roiling darkness glided silently across the room and snaked its way towards the two women. Its cold, ethereal fingers reached out towards Mia's, hoping to sink its dark tendrils into her very being.

As the spirit's hand drew near, however, it recoiled violently, repelled by the intricate sigils that adorned Mia's body. It tried a second time, but was immediately repelled again. A snarl of frustration echoed through the otherwise silent room as the spirit realized it could not possess the young witch.

But the spirit would not be deterred so easily. The witch was a threat, but the blonde one? She was *his*.

Riley shuddered in her sleep, her face contorting with unease as the spirit wormed its way into her mind, invading her thoughts and memories. Her consciousness retreated into the furthest reaches of her psyche, leaving behind a vacant shell for the spirit to inhabit. As the possession took hold, Riley's eyes flickered open, revealing a cold, unnatural stare that bore no resemblance to her usual warm gaze.

"Ah, yes," the spirit murmured through Riley's lips, testing out the physical form it now controlled. "This will do nicely." Savoring the sensation of a living body, the spirit turned its attention back to Mia, still peacefully asleep and unaware of the danger lurking beside her. The witch had been in his house, and the witch could hurt him. The witch needed to be eliminated.

Riley's body moved with unnatural fluidity, silently rising in the bed while her breathing remained slow and steady. The possessing spirit, now in control of her every action, allowed its eerie gaze to sweep over Mia's sleeping form. A sinister smile spread across Riley's face as the spirit reveled in the vulnerability of its prey.

"Such a fragile thing," it whispered through Riley's lips in a tone as cold as ice.

As if on cue, Riley's hand shot out, clamping around Mia's throat with an iron grip. The sudden attack jolted Mia from her sleep, her eyes flying open in terror. Gasping for breath, she looked up into the cold, blue eyes of her possessed friend, realizing with horror what exactly was happening.

"Ri-Riley?" she choked out, her heart pounding in her chest as she struggled against the vice-like grip. But it wasn't Riley who stared back at her.

"Your friend isn't here right now," the spirit sneered, tightening its hold on Mia's throat. "And soon, you won't be either."

"Bullshit," Mia squeaked out. Her vision began to blur as she did her best to keep panic from consuming her. She had to come up with a plan, and she needed to come up with it fast. She had to find a way to stop this thing without hurting Riley. Clinging to the last vestiges of her consciousness, Mia's thoughts raced, desperate to find a way out.

"Fight him, Riley," Mia whispered, her voice barely audible beneath the crushing pressure on her windpipe. "Don't let him win."

The spirit laughed, a chilling sound that sent tremors of dread down Mia's spine. "She can't hear you," it taunted. "She belongs to me now."

Mia's heart was banging like a jackhammer, adrenaline coursing through her veins as she fought to stay conscious. She silently slid her hand down to her right thigh hoping the spirit wouldn't notice, and began to trace one of the sigils slowly with her finger. As it glowed with its activation, Mia willed a shimmering shield of protection into existence, surrounding her and knocking Riley's body onto its back.

"Wha–?" the vengeful spirit snarled, confusion flickering across Riley's face as it tried to comprehend the barrier that blocked its sinister intentions.

"Get out of her!" Mia commanded, her voice resonating with raw anger. "This is the one time I say it nicely!"

Silence filled the room for a moment, only to be shattered by the spirit's sinister laughter. "Weak little things, you think you scare me?" it taunted. "You are fragile toys for me to play with and nothing more."

Mia's jaw clenched, her dark brown eyes blazing with defiance. "Nothing fragile about me right now," she hissed, her voice rasping in the dark. "I will protect her at any cost."

The spirit regarded her coldly, Riley's blue eyes devoid of emotion. "We shall see," it whispered ominously, lunging forward once more.

As the possessed Riley collided with the magical barrier, Mia poured every ounce of her strength into maintaining the shield around her. She knew she had to act quickly before the spirit could gain the upper hand again. The room seemed to vibrate with the intensity of their struggle, and Mia's heart raced as she frantically searched for a solution.

"Riley, listen to me," she urged, her voice strained by the effort it took to keep the barrier intact. "I know you can hear me. I'm going to get you out of this, but I need you to keep fighting him. Do everything you can to loosen his control."

"Your words are meaningless," the spirit growled through Riley's lips. "She lives in my house. She's a Blackwood now, and you can't steal her away from me."

"You are the most cliched jackass I've met yet, and I've tangled with literal demons," Mia spat, defiance lacing her words.

"Such brave words, little witch," the spirit mocked, flexing Riley's hands into claws. "But let's see how long your courage lasts."

Without warning, the possessed Riley lunged at the shimmering barrier surrounding Mia, striking with an otherworldly shriek. After getting knocked back, Riley's body launched itself at Mia again. And again. The thing was using Riley's body like a battering ram against Mia's barrier.

The force behind the attack rattled Mia's resolve, her concern shifting from her own safety to Riley's. She honestly wasn't sure how much more abuse Riley's body could take before she started to sustain real injury.

Mia kicked into overdrive. She glanced around the room, her eyes darting between the various objects scattered about. Her heart raced as she mentally cataloged the items she needed for an exorcism ritual. Only a few of her sigils were charged right now, which meant she was going to need components to supplement them.

"Stay strong, Riley," Mia whispered under her breath. "I'll save you."

Diving across the darkened room, she quickly pulled a bundle of dried lavender out of a small wooden box on her shelf, and then grabbed a sharpie off of her desk.

"Let's get to work," she muttered, focusing on the task at hand.

Using the marker, Mia began inscribing a new sigil on the ground. Her fingers moved deftly, tracing symbols imbued with her own energy. The air around the symbols seemed to crackle with energy.

"Riley, I need you to listen to me," she said, her voice laced with urgency. "This is really going to suck."

As if in response, the possessed Riley let out a guttural growl, baring her teeth. But Mia could see a flicker of fear behind those wild eyes – the real Riley, pleading for help.

"Give in," the spirit hissed through Riley's lips. "You know what you're doing might kill her, Mia."

"Not if I do it correctly," Mia replied, anger and fear mingling in her voice. "I won't let you take her!"

"Then let me have you instead," the spirit offered, its words dripping with malice. "You know how good it feels, don't you?"

Mia's breath hitched as the temptation clawed at her mind. The euphoric high of demonic possession beckoned her like a siren call, promising power and pleasure beyond her wildest dreams. Ghosts weren't quite the same, but it would be something. It would feel enough like it. The thrill would pass through her, the ecstasy of another being's will pulsing through her...

But she couldn't. Not again. And there was no way this thing would let Riley go willingly even if she did.

"Nice pitch, but no, chucklefuck," Mia said defiantly. "Enjoy the eviction."

Mia triggered a minor rune on her left hand, igniting the bundle of lavender. The smoke began to fill the room, and drift towards Riley. Soon it surrounded her possessed form.

"Do you think that can hurt me?" the spirit sneered. "You're weak. Just a broken little witch."

"That's not the spell," Mia smirked. "That's just the medium." She focused her energy, channeling it into a powerful burst of magic aimed directly at the possessed Riley. "K'veh m'xex rhi'annos!"

The room tremored as arcs of energy danced from Mia through the burning lavender's smoke, snaking into Riley's body.

"You think this can hurt me?" the spirit taunted, as Riley's body began to violently shake. "I thought you were stronger than this, witch."

"What, you think I'd just let you finish immediately?" Mia spat. "Best experiences take more than a minute, sweetie."

Mia snapped her fingers, and the rest of the energy in the air collapsed into Riley's body, lifting it off of the floor. The spirit released one final, blood-curdling scream before being torn from Riley's shaking body. As the young professor dropped to the floor, Mia immediately crossed the distance to catch her.

"Riley?" Mia whispered, her chest heaving with exertion and relief. "Can you hear me?"

"Y-yeah," Riley choked out, her eyes still glazed with fear. "I'm not dreaming? What... how did that happen?"

Mia's body trembled with exhaustion, the adrenaline from the encounter leaving her system in rapid waves. The room spun around her as she tightened her grip on Riley, trying to ground herself. Her muscles ached from the strain of maintaining the protective barrier and performing the exorcism, but she couldn't afford to let go just yet.

"I think we just met Mason Blackwood."

Chapter 14

The room was heavy with the scent of burnt lavender and sweat, a haze of exhaustion settling over Mia's slumped shoulders. In the dim light, Riley's bruises seemed to glow against her pale skin – angry purples and blues that screamed of Mason Blackwood's malevolence.

"Damn," Riley muttered, gingerly touching her tender jaw, wincing at the pain. "He really did a number on me."

"That was too close," Mia breathed, her voice ragged from energy she had just shoved through her body. Her dark brown eyes glittered with determination, but her body trembled with fatigue. "We can't let him get this close again."

Riley nodded, her eyes examining the wreckage and upturned furniture that littered Mia's small apartment. "Yeah, not a fan."

"He's more powerful than I thought. I've read about ghosts that weren't bound to a physical location, but I've never seen it before. This guy is mobile, and that means a lot of the normal rules don't apply," Mia said shaking her head. "I wanted to take my time, to be careful… but I don't think we can. He's forcing my hand. We're going to have to take drastic action."

"Drastic action" tasted dangerous on Mia's tongue, but she knew it was necessary. The adrenaline still coursed through her veins, fueling her resolve. "Mason Blackwood is the most powerful spirit I've directly encountered. We don't have time for me to sit and research for weeks. We can't wait."

Riley nodded, getting to her feet and turning on the room's single lamp.

"We're going to have to use it," Mia began, her voice low and tinged with trepidation, "We're going to have to use the nuclear option."

"Are we still calling it that?" Riley raised an eyebrow, her voice laced with sarcasm but also a hint of genuine curiosity. "You need to give it a better name."

"Funny. But calling it 'Iggatol's Grand Banishing' kind of undersells it," Mia replied.

"Okay, fair," Riley shrugged. "What makes it necessary though?"

"Getting rid of Blackwood isn't like banishing a common ghost," Mia explained, picking at the frayed edge of her tanktop. "I think he's been drawing from the energy of everyone who's ever died in your house. I've never seen a spirit with this kind of power before."

"So yeah," Riley murmured, swallowing hard. "That sounds terrifying."

"Terrifying is an understatement," Mia admitted, her fingers curling into fists. "Normally you just need to kick a ghost out of a space, and they lose all their power. Kicking *this* asshole out of that house would just piss him off, and he'd just attack you anywhere *other* than the house."

"That's not exactly ideal," Riley agreed.

"So we can't just banish him from the house, but from this entire plane of existence," Mia explained. "And he's not going to go willingly. He has the strength of *dozens* behind him, and it's just my focused will against all of that. I'm going to need to channel so much energy that we'll be walking a fine line. If we don't get the ritual absolutely right, it could leave me powerless."

"Powerless..." Riley echoed, her gaze flickering to the protective sigils tattooed on Mia's arms. "Could you really live without your magic, Mia?"

"He's killed people. He's going to kill more. My magic isn't worth anyone's life," Mia said resolutely, her eyes burning with determination.

Riley watched Mia's face, awe mingling with concern. "I appreciate your willingness to protect me, Mia, but I don't want you to lose yourself in the process. Are you absolutely sure this is something you're willing to do?"

Mia looked into Riley's anxious eyes, her own reflecting a steadfast resolve. "I know the risks, but getting rid of Mason Blackwood is crucial. We can't let him continue to torment you or anyone else. It didn't stop with Lila Rose, and it's not going to stop with you unless we make it." Her fingers brushed gently against Riley's bruised wrist, and she felt a shiver run down her spine. "We're in this together, okay?"

"Okay," Riley agreed quietly, her confident tone betrayed by a slight waver in her voice.

"First things first though, we are *not* letting tonight's events happen a second time," Mia said. "I'm going to make you something." Mia started scrounging around the chaos that covered the small desk in the corner, rummaging through its drawers and tossing its contents out in a flurry. In the end, Mia produced a small piece of obsidian on a silver chain, and began to carefully etch a symbol into the volcanic glass.

"Now I have this tattooed on me, but I'm also a weirdo who does weird things," Mia said, bent over the desk. "I'm going to give you the conventional version of this spell in a talisman."

With a small glow of energy flowing from a sigil on Mia's hand, the piece of obsidian seemed to pulse for a moment, before returning to its natural black. Mia walked over to Riley and looped the chain around her neck.

"This will prevent anything from possessing you that you don't voluntarily let in," Mia said. "I wish I did this earlier, but I really didn't think he could leave the property. Because, again, that's not a thing that happens."

"Thank you, Mia," Riley whispered. "I hope you know how much I appreciate this."

Mia smiled softly, the warmth of the sentiment reaching her eyes. "I'll keep that in mind the next time I can't make rent."

"Now to do something I should have done a month ago when I first moved in." With a determined nod, Mia grabbed a knife from the kitchenette, and approached the nearest wall. "This is going to make me lose my deposit when I move out down the road..."

"What are you doing exactly?" Riley asked.

"Watch closely," Mia instructed, as she began carving a series of intricate sigils into the plaster, her movements fluid and deliberate. "These symbols will cloak the space from supernatural beings, making it nearly impossible for them to find us while we're in here. I didn't think to do it originally since I live alone and my tattoos protect me. I got over confident."

"What, you didn't think 'hey, I might bring someone cute home some time and I need to keep them safe?'" Riley asked teasingly.

"Honestly, you were the first person I brought home since I moved here," Mia shrugged. "I've only lived in town for like a month. The one hookup I had here before you I went to her place."

Riley leaned in, her gaze locked on the twisting patterns emerging under Mia's deft touch. She recognized some of the sigils from Mia's tattoos, and a shiver ran down her spine at the realization of just how vulnerable they were without such protection.

"So how do these symbols work?" Riley asked, her voice barely above a whisper, not wanting to disturb Mia's focus.

"The sigils layer on each other, reinforcing the spell. Don't think of them as two dimensional symbols, but instead multidimensional structures, and what end up on the wall is just the point where they intercept the surface I'm carving them in," Mia explained, her voice a soft hum as she continued her work. "Some repel dark forces, while others strengthen the protective barriers. Most importantly they hide the apartment, making it appear like it doesn't even exist. It's like weaving a tapestry of energy to keep us safe."

"Will it be enough?" The question slipped from Riley's lips before she could stop herself.

"Nothing is guaranteed in our world," Mia admitted, pausing for a moment to assess her handiwork. "But I'm doing everything I can to stack the odds in our favor. And, on the upside, this should work on *any* supernatural beings – not just ghosts."

"So like demons and stuff," Riley nodded.

"Yeah, exactly, And that 'stuff' is a pretty long list," Mia affirmed, "They would walk right by, wouldn't even able to see the door."

As the last sigil took form under Mia's expert hand, Riley felt a shiver run down her spine. The room seemed to vibrate with energy, the air crackling with an almost palpable sense of power. She could feel it down to her bones. Something had shifted, something had changed.

"Is it done?" she whispered, her voice barely audible over the hum of magic that now filled the space.

Mia nodded, wiping the sweat from her brow as she surveyed her handiwork. "It is," she confirmed, her tone heavy with the weight of that night's events. "And now, we prepare for the battle ahead."

"Okay." Riley paused, swallowing hard. "What's our next move?"

"Well, the first step is getting some sleep, because I'm tired as hell," Mia began, her voice finally revealing the extent of her exhaustion. "But after that we need to gather the materials for the banishing spell. I've got a list." She pulled a small notepad from one of the many stacks, handing it to Riley with a determined gleam in her dark eyes.

"Is one of the items on this list a live mouse?" Riley asked, an eyebrow raised in incredulity.

"Yeah we can skip that. Iggatol tosses a few ingredients in you don't actually need. He was an overdramatic ceremonial magician and contemporary of Crowley, except his spells *actually* work," Mia replied, a hint of amusement dancing in her eyes amidst the seriousness of their situation. "We can also skip anything that starts with 'a lover's' this or 'a virgin's' that."

"Good to know. So, how do we find these items? I don't exactly have a pantry full of magical ingredients," Riley admitted with a dry chuckle.

"I mean, *I* do though. The rest are literally for sale at the shop. We're literally doing a 50% off sale on herbs starting tomorrow," Mia said, her lips curling into a devious smile. "But again, the first order is sleep though. It's three A.M., and both of us have to go to work in the morning."

"Screw that, I got possessed," Riley said shaking her head. "I'm calling in sick."

Chapter 15

Mia's eyelids grew heavy as Riley's rhythmic snores filled the small apartment. She could feel her body sinking deeper into the uneven mattress, the cotton sheets caressing her skin as she surrendered to slumber. The world around her seemed to blur, sensations blending together until her consciousness slipped away entirely.

The transition from reality to dream was seamless, and at first, Mia was unaware that anything had changed. As her mind registered the shift in surroundings, a faint sense of unease settled in the pit of her stomach. Gone were the familiar trappings of her bedroom, replaced by the unfamiliar apartment filled with Sarah's belongings she had seen in her dream the other day. Personal items were scattered across dark wooden shelves, things that had once been both of theirs that Mia had left far behind.

"Sarah?" Mia called out hesitantly, her voice echoing through the silent space. The only response was a low creaking sound, as if the floorboards were groaning beneath her weight.

"Great, I'm in the creepy dream version of this place. Where the hell did my subconscious come up with this stuff," she wondered aloud, her breath catching as she noticed something peculiar about the apartment: it seemed to be pulsating, as though it were alive. The hairs on the back of her neck stood up, sending shivers down her spine. *God I shouldn't do magic right before going to bed, it fucks me up something bad*, she thought, her intuition whispering a warning that something wasn't quite right.

Mia hesitated for a moment, her eyes drawn to a chair piled high with weapons she had never seen before, including a long silver dagger. An uneasy feeling settled in her stomach.

"Sarah?" Mia called out tentatively, her voice barely above a whisper. Her heart pounded in her chest, and she could feel her pulse racing in anticipation of what might come next.

As if summoned by the desperation in Mia's plea, Sarah materialized from the shadows, her gaze intense and unyielding. Every muscle in her body seemed coiled and ready to strike. The tension in the room was palpable as Sarah moved with the grace of a caged tiger. Her hair looked like it did in the other dream, and she seemed more muscular than Mia remembered.

But it was Sarah.

"God, not this again, why are you here? Why can't I just forget about you?" Sarah asked, her tone sharp and biting.

"I, umm... good to see you too–" Mia stammered, taken aback by the other woman's aggression.

"Save it," Sarah snapped, cutting her off. "Why are you here? Why is *this* happening."

Mia hesitated, weighing her words carefully. God, the real Sarah probably hated her this much too. *Why can't I look at memories with rose tinted glasses like everyone else?*

"I don't know why I'm here either," Mia admitted, her voice trembling slightly. "There's something happening, something dangerous, and I don't know what to do."

"Of course you don't," Sarah remarked bitterly, her eyes narrowing. "You always were good at getting in over your head."

"It's not my fault this time," Mia explained. "She asked for my help, was I supposed to say no and just let her die?"

For a moment, the tension seemed to waver as Sarah regarded her with a mix of curiosity and suspicion. She circled Mia slowly, her movements deliberate and calculated, assessing the sincerity of her words.

"Fine," she finally conceded, her voice low and guarded. "Tell me what's going on, but make it quick. I don't have time for your games."

"I made a new friend," Mia began, her voice trembling slightly, "Someone from outside our world. And she's in serious danger. There's something in her house."

Sarah's eyes narrowed, but the hostility in her expression softened just a fraction, replaced by an edge of concern. "Tell me more," she urged, her voice still guarded yet tinged with curiosity.

Mia took a deep breath, and as she recounted the events of Riley's perilous situation, she couldn't help but shudder at the thought of what could happen if she failed to intervene. "I have to cast a spell," she continued, her words coming out in a rush. "A massively powerful one to save her. But if I fail, my magic will be severed permanently."

As Mia spoke, she could see Sarah's demeanor shifting, the initial animosity giving way to understanding. Her eyes softened, and her body language relaxed as she moved to sit down next to Mia, the tension between them slowly dissipating.

"God, Mia," Sarah murmured, her gaze sympathetic, "that sounds terrifying. How are you holding up?"

Tears welled up in Mia's eyes as she confessed her deepest fears. "I'm scared, Sarah. More scared than I've ever been. What if I can't do this? What if I lose everything? What if I fail, lose my magic, *and* the ghost still takes her."

Silence stretched out between them, punctuated only by the creaking floorboards and eerie shadows cast by the dim light. For a moment, it seemed as though Sarah might revert back to her hostile stance, but instead, she placed a gentle hand on Mia's shoulder.

"I sound so selfish," Mia whispered. "You gave up so much more than that to save me."

"I don't regret anything I did to keep you safe and alive," Sarah said softly, her voice determined yet compassionate. "You know I wanted you to stop doing magic. But I want it to be because you choose it, not because you're forced to. You're stronger than you give yourself credit for, Mia Graves. I know you can handle this."

Mia took a deep breath, her fingers twisting the fabric of her skirt. With Sarah's softened gaze fixed upon her, she felt a sense of urgency to mend what had been broken between them even if this was just a dream.

"Sarah," she began, her voice wavering with the weight of her guilt, "there's something I need to tell you. Something I never had the courage to actually tell you." She paused, searching for the right words. "I'm sorry. I abandoned you and left you to deal with what happened to you on your own."

The apology hung in the air, heavy and oppressive like the shadows that crept around the room. Mia could feel her heart beating wildly in her chest, a cacophony of longing and remorse threatening to consume her.

"God, if only I had been there for you when you needed me most," Mia continued, tears welling up in her eyes. "We were supposed to face it together, but I ran away. I was so scared, and I didn't know how to help either of us."

Sarah remained silent, her expression unreadable as she absorbed Mia's desperate words. The tension in the room tightened, each creaking floorboard an echo of the distance that had grown between them.

"Please, can you ever forgive me?" Mia implored, the vulnerability in her voice making her seem smaller, more fragile than ever before.

For a moment, it seemed as though the entire world held its breath, waiting for Sarah's response. And then, with a sigh she spoke.

"I don't know Mia," she admitted softly, her eyes shimmering with unshed tears. "But I'd want to try. God I wish we were really sitting together."

Sarah's gaze softened as she took in Mia's tear-streaked face, her heart aching at the vulnerability laid bare before her. The hostility that had once gripped her seemed to dissipate like smoke on the wind, replaced instead by a weary resignation.

"Sometimes I wonder if I'm the dream, and you're the one who's real," Sarah mused, her voice barely above a whisper. "If only the real Mia was this open with me... I might actually be able to forgive her."

Mia's breath hitched in her throat, a torrent of emotions surging through her. Regret weighed heavy on her soul as she realized how much she'd held back from Sarah in the past. If they'd been able to communicate like this earlier, perhaps things could have been different.

"God, I wish I had been," she murmured, her eyes downcast. "I wish I'd let you in more. I wish I was brave enough to say this to the actual Sarah."

"Regrets will always weigh us down, but we can't let them," Sarah said gently, her warm brown eyes inviting

Mia to meet her gaze. "I don't know if you're real or I'm real, so let me tell you this – I miss you every day. I'm still pissed as hell at you, but I also hope you're okay."

"I miss you too, and I still love you," Mia said quietly. "I wish I'd been strong enough to stay."

Mia and Sarah sat together for a moment, the eerie shadows and whispers of the decaying apartment feeling less scary by the moment.

"So, uh, is this where you live now?" Mia asked cautiously. "Like I'm concerned that this is where my subconscious thinks you're living."

"God, I swear it's nicer in real life," Sarah said shaking her head. "But yeah."

"It's bigger than my place, so that's something," Mia laughed. "I just–" The world began to fade away from Mia, like sand slipping between fingers. "I think I'm waking up, Sarah."

"Good luck, Mia," Sarah said quietly. "And I love you too."

The last vestiges of the dream vanished, leaving Mia suspended in darkness for a moment before reality crashed down upon her. The comforting softness of her bed brought her back to the waking world, the faint sound of Riley's snores next to her bringing a sense of normalcy.

Blinking open her heavy eyes, Mia stared at the ceiling, her mind racing as she tried to reconcile the fading memories of her dream with the reality that now enveloped her. The emotional intensity of her conversation with Sarah still clung to her, a persistent ache in her chest that refused to dissipate.

Mia turned over and closed her eyes to find sleep once again. Every dream of Sarah brought an ocean of regret, but a small comfort she could cling to as well.

Chapter 16

Riley's house seemed to loom at the end of the street, a dark and foreboding presence even in the stark daylight. The Victorian architecture of the large house cast ominous shadows across the front yard, while the faint whispers of wind through the trees seemed to hint at the secrets hidden within the walls. The eerie atmosphere sent shivers down Riley's spine as she realized that soon they would have to confront the malevolent spirit haunting her home.

"Ready to get this done?" Mia asked, clutching her satchel of tools tightly.

"As ready as I can be," Riley replied, her voice wavering slightly despite her best efforts to remain stoic. She took a deep breath, trying to focus on the task ahead rather than the fear gnawing at her insides.

"Remember, get angry not scared," Mia said. "Not being afraid weakens what he can do to you. It won't *stop* him, but it's not nothing."

"Easier said than done," Riley said with a glance to Mia.

"Yeah, but I gotta keep saying it." Mia led the way into through the front door, past the foyer, and into the living room. Her steps were resolute but cautious, almost as if the floor itself was unsteady. She pulled up the rugs, revealing the bare wooden floor beneath, and began to inscribe large sigils in chalk upon the floorboards.

"Hand me the lavender, please," Mia requested, not looking away from her task. Riley passed her a pouch of herbs, watching as Mia incorporated it into the intricate design she was creating.

"Tell me again how this is supposed to work," Riley asked, her mind racing with a mix of doubt and hope. She needed to understand, to believe that they could succeed against the vengeful spirit of Mason Blackwood.

Mia paused, meeting her gaze. "These sigils will channel energy through me, allowing me to tap into enough power to banish him from reality. There are lay lines that intersect about five miles from here in the middle of a cornfield, so I'm going to tap into the residual energy generated by that. But I need to be careful – if I lose control for even a moment, I am absolutely screwed."

"What if he comes out before we're ready?" Riley asked, handing Mia another piece of chalk. "He mostly stayed in the basement during the day last time, but that's not a guarantee of anything. What if he notices?"

"Then I'll need you to improvise," Mia replied, her dark eyes narrowed in concentration as she completed another sigil. She blew away the excess chalk dust, watching as the intricate patterns began to glow with a faint, ethereal light. "Riley," Mia said suddenly, her voice tense. "Do you hear that?"

Riley strained her ears, listening for any sound out of the ordinary. At first, all she could hear was the pounding of her own heart, but then she caught it: a low, sinister creaking, like old bones shifting beneath the weight of centuries.

"Basement stairs," Riley breathed, white-knuckling the obsidian pendant Mia had made for her. The malevolent presence they'd been dreading loomed closer, announcing itself with each step Mason Blackwood took. There was a thickness to the air, and a chill ran down Riley's back.

"Keep working on the spell," Riley told Mia, her voice trembling but resolute. "I'll distract him, lead him away."

"Are you sure?" Mia asked, her face etched with concern.

"No, but what the hell else am I going to do?" Riley replied, forcing herself to sound confident. She knew she had to be the bait if they had any hope of banishing Mason Blackwood for good.

"Be careful," Mia warned as Riley slipped out of the living room.

Riley's heart was pounding in her chest as she crept through the house, trying to move as silently as possible. She didn't want Blackwood to know where she came from and accidentally lead him to Mia. When she reached the entrance to the basement, she hesitated for a moment, gazing into the darkness below. Riley took a deep breath, steeled her nerves, and threw the door open with a crash.

"Hey, Blackwood!" she shouted, her voice echoing through the gloom. "Looking for me?"

She didn't have to wait long for a response. A chilling gust of wind whipped past her face, carrying with it the scent of decay and rage. It was him – Mason Blackwood was on the hunt.

"Come and get me, asshole!" Riley taunted, turning on her heel and sprinting through the house. She could feel him close behind. She didn't need to stay ahead of him for too long though.

She just needed to buy Mia time.

****

Mia worked as quickly as she could, the sounds of Riley's taunts echoing through the house. What Riley was doing was dangerous, but they didn't really have another choice right now. The chalk screeched against the floorboards as she finished inscribing the complex sigils of the spell, her hands shaking with adrenaline. There was no room for error now; every line had to be perfect.

"X'noth, mqu'ay," Mia whispered, her voice low but firm. "th'lin vi'ondra."

As she spoke the words, she felt a surge of energy flow through her veins, traveling from her core to the tips of her fingers and toes. Her tattoos began to glow, pulsing with the trickle of raw, untamed power. It was a careful dance, and she needed to keep the tempo.

"You can do this," she muttered to herself, clenching her fists and channeling the energy into her sigils. "You have to."

As the power built, she became aware of a shift in the atmosphere. The spirits of the Rose House, victims of Mason Blackwood's rage, began to gather in the living room around Mia, their ghostly forms flickering like candle flames. They watched her with curiosity and awe, sensing the immense power she wielded.

"Hey guys, stay back," Mia warned them, her voice barely more than a whisper. "I don't want to hurt you, and if you get too close you might get caught in the middle of what I'm doing."

The spirits seemed to understand, keeping their distance but continuing to observe the ritual. Every single spirit here had likely had their lives ended by Blackwood over the years, and even in death he still terrorized them.

They had as much skin in the game as anyone else.

The power kept building, flowing into Mia. She felt as if she were standing in the eye of a hurricane, the power swirling around her like a tempest, threatening to consume her if she made one wrong move.

****

Riley's heart raced as she darted through the dimly lit hallway on the second floor. Blackwood was close on her heels, and she had to keep him occupied. The sinister laughter echoing behind her only confirmed her fear.

"Come now little girl, you cannot run forever," Blackwood taunted, his voice like the grinding of malevolent glass.

Crouching behind a dusty old dresser, Riley clutched the obsidian pendant Mia had given her. Cool in her hand, she hoped the spell Mia bound into it would keep her safe.

"Ah, there you are," he snarled, bursting into the room and tossing the dresser aside. What stood before Riley wasn't a man, but two blazing eyes of fire swarmed by smoke.

In that instant, Riley felt a sudden surge of power from the pendant, shielding her from Mason's attempt to possess her. She could see his fury intensify as realization dawned on him – he no longer had control over her. It was now or never.

"Is that all you've got, Mason?" Riley spat, defiance replacing the fear in her voice. She knew she needed to buy Mia more time, even if it meant putting herself in more danger.

"Insolent child!" Mason roared, his rage palpable. He lunged at her, pushing her back with a supernatural strength that sent her crashing through a door into another room. Splinters of wood flew around her as she stumbled, but she refused to let that stop her. She scrambled to her feet bloodied and bruised and continued her desperate flight, making her way towards the attic.

"Your pathetic attempts to evade me are futile!" Mason bellowed, his anger growing with each passing moment. "You'll never get away!"

As Riley climbed the creaky attic stairs, she couldn't help but wonder if this was truly her last stand.

But if it was, it was going to be worth it.

****

Mia stood at the center of the chalk sigils, her eyes closed in concentration. She could feel the energy pulsing beneath her feet, like a heartbeat echoing through the floorboards. The air crackled with the electric charge of power, causing the hair on her arms to stand on end.

"Come on, Mia," she whispered, her voice barely audible above the hum. "You can do this."

She moved her hands slowly, drawing upon the energy harnessed within her tattoos. The power surged upwards, connecting her with the sigils on the floor. In response, the floorboards began to shake and glow, as if they were alive.

"Find the balance point," Mia said quietly to herself, willing the chaos around her to coalesce into something more controlled. "Find the balance point."

As she channeled her energy into the ritual, beads of sweat formed on her forehead. The intensity of the power coursing through her was unlike anything she had ever experienced. It threatened to consume her, to overwhelm her senses and leave her vulnerable to the darkness that still lingered at the edges of her mind.

"Are you sure this will work?" asked a small, hesitant voice from behind her. Mia glanced over her shoulder to see the spirit of the young boy she'd met the other day, worry and wonder shining in his eyes.

Ben, his name was Ben.

"Nothing is certain," Mia admitted, her voice laced with determination. "But I have to try."

"I hope you succeed, we all do," the spirit said, nodding to the others who stood by in silent support.

"Thanks, dead kid," Mia breathed, returning her focus to the task at hand. She knew that every second counted. The longer it took her to complete the ritual, the more danger Riley faced.

"Channel the energy," she muttered, forcing her hands to remain steady as the floorboards continued to shake, the sigils glowing brighter with each passing moment. "Find the balance point."

"Save Riley," she added in an urgent whisper, feeling a newfound surge of determination flood through her veins.

****

The attic was cloaked in shadows, its air thick and stifling. Riley tried to keep panic at bay as she frantically searched for a way out. She could sense Mason Blackwood's spirit closing in, his rage filled presence growing stronger by the second.

"Damn it," Riley muttered through gritted teeth, her heart pounding in her chest. The obsidian pendant around her neck felt cold against her skin, but just because he couldn't possess her didn't mean he couldn't hurt her.

"Where are you, little one?" Blackwood's voice echoed through the attic, a sinister laugh laced with venom. "You can't run forever."

"Think, think, think," Riley whispered to herself, eyes darting around the cluttered space, searching for any weapon or means of escape. Her breath came in ragged gasps, lungs burning from exertion and fear.

In that moment, Blackwood materialized before her, his spirit a swirling mass of darkness and rage. He lunged at her, and Riley barely managed to dodge his grasp. She stumbled back, tripping over a stack of old boxes, and found herself cornered, pinned against the wall.

"Got you," Blackwood sneered, his ghostly form looming over her like a specter of death itself. "Nowhere left to run, little girl."

"Leave me alone!" Riley shouted, defiance flaring within her despite the terror gripping her heart. She braced herself for the inevitable strike, but it never came.

"Get away from her!" Lila Rose's voice rang out like a battle cry, her ghostly form suddenly appearing between Riley and Blackwood. Her eyes blazed with fury, her once seductive aura replaced by one of sheer determination.

"Now now, you shouldn't be out and about, dear," Mason snarled, his attention momentarily diverted. "Go back to bed for when papa is ready."

"You don't control me anymore, and I won't let you harm anyone else," Lila retorted, her voice dripping with venom.

Before he could respond, Lila unleashed an unearthly scream, her rage manifesting as a shockwave of energy that sent Mason's spirit reeling backward.

"Go!" Lila shouted, turning to Riley. "Get out of here!"

Riley didn't hesitate. She scrambled to her feet and darted past the writhing form of Mason Blackwood, his anger-filled howls echoing through the attic.

****

Mia's hands trembled as she activated the final sigil, sweat dripping down her brow. The raw power coursing through her veins threatened to consume her, but she refused to give in. This was it. This was as far as she could go. She had taken more energy into her than she had ever dreamt possible, and with the spirits of the house watching, Mia knew it was time to send both it and Mason Blackwood to their final destination.

"Here goes nothing," Mia said, clasping her hands together. With all of her remaining willpower, she directed the flow of energy towards one, single thought. One single target.

Mason Blackwood.

The ground beneath her feet shook violently, as if the house itself were reacting to the sheer force of the spell. A brilliant pulse of light surged from the chalk-drawn sigils, its radiance cascading through the air like a tidal wave of pure energy.

Up in the attic, Riley watched in awe as the searing light engulfed Mason Blackwood, his rage-filled form contorted in agony. His spirit writhed in torment, unable to escape the spell's merciless grasp.

"NO!" he screamed, his voice barely audible over the cacophony of the spell's climax. "This is not the end! You can't stop me!"

But his threat fell on deaf ears. With one final, gut-wrenching scream, Mason Blackwood exploded into countless shards of light and shadow, his essence scattered to the winds. In that instant, the oppressive darkness that had hung over the house lifted, replaced by an almost palpable sense of relief.

Riley collapsed onto the attic floor, her body trembling with adrenaline and exhaustion. "You did it, Mia," she whispered, tears streaming down her cheeks. "You really did it."

Riley felt a cool breeze near her ear.

"You look exhausted dear," Lila said quietly. "You should rest for a moment."

Chapter 17

"Riley! Are you okay? I'm coming up!" Mia shouted, her footsteps echoing on the wooden stairs.

"Be careful," Riley's voice rang out. "There's a lot of damage up here."

As Mia emerged into the dim attic, her expression shifted from concern to awe at the sight of their victory's aftermath. The destroyed remains of old furniture and boxes were scattered across the space, like the fallout of some grand battle. She approached Riley, who winced as she gingerly probed her bruised ribs.

"Are you hurt?" Mia asked, her dark eyes filled with worry.

"Nothing that won't heal," Riley assured her, forcing a weak smile. "What matters is you stopped him."

"I'm sorry I wasn't faster," Mia murmured, looking at Riley with concern. "I'm sorry you had to be alone..."

"I wasn't alone," Riley smiled, leaning on Mia for support. "Lila Rose helped me, though it seems she's gone back into hiding. I think it took a lot out of her."

"Well we should thank her when we see her next," Mia nodded.

"Maybe she'll move on now," Riley suggested, her thoughts drifting to the other spirits in the house. "Along with all the others."

Mia nodded solemnly. "I don't know. Blackwood exploited them, and even killed a lot of them... but I don't think he had the power to keep them from moving on."

"Too bad," Riley said quietly. "I was hoping they'd find peace."

"They still might," Mia replied. "But I think that's a bit beyond our control."

Mia and Riley made their way back down to the house's living room and promptly collapsed onto the sofa.

Riley let out a deep, shuddering sigh as she leaned back against the soft cushions. For the first time since moving into this haunted house, she felt truly safe within its walls. "We did it," Riley whispered, her disbelief evident.

Mia chuckled weakly, her dark eyes glancing around the room, taking in the absolute mess she'd made of the place. "Yeah, we sure did," she agreed, her body aching from the raw energy that had just ripped through it.

A momentary silence fell between the two, both trying to regain their composure after facing off against the vengeful ghost. Their gazes wandered across the scattered debris of their confrontation: overturned furniture, shattered glass, and the spent sigils that had been drawn hastily upon the wooden floor.

"Maybe we should just put the carpets back and cover up the used sigils," Mia suggested, her tone laced with humor and exhaustion. "A little interior redecoration never hurt anyone."

"Or you could grab a bucket and mop instead," Riley retorted, a playful smile tugging at the corners of her lips despite the weariness etched on her face. "I don't want you accidentally activating some random spell when you stop by six months from now."

Their laughter filled the room, chasing away the remaining shadows cast by Mason Blackwood's presence.

Mia let a soft chuckle as she turned to Riley. "You know," she began, her voice tinged with vulnerability, "I've been alone for the last year. I was kind of shut down. It's been... nice to have someone need me again."

"Since Jake left me, I've been feeling alone too. He kind of got all of our friends in the breakup, and all of my family is on the west coast," Riley admitted, her fingers tracing an absent pattern on the armrest of the couch. "It's been nice having an actual friend again, y'know... minus the evil ghost trying to kill us."

"Well I've never met him, but Jake sounds like a piece of human garbage," Mia nodded quietly. "You deserve better."

"The biggest problem is I still miss him," Riley sighed. "We bought this giant house to start a family in, and now it's just me."

"I mean, there are all the ghosts," Mia smirked. "You have plenty of roommates."

"True," Riley laughed. "Very true. And if I haven't said it enough – thank you, Mia. For everything."

"Likewise," Mia replied, her dark eyes shimmering with sincerity. "We make a pretty good team, don't we?"

"Damn right, we do," Riley affirmed. "I bet you're gonna miss having me crash in your apartment and steal your sheets."

Mia's laughter bubbled up, soft and genuine, the warmth of it spreading through the room. "I'll admit, having someone else around was kind of nice." She brushed a stray curl from her face, her eyes meeting Riley's in quiet camaraderie.

Riley glanced around the grand living room, its cavernous space suddenly feeling bright and open now that Mason Blackwood's spirit was gone. "This house is so big, empty... you could always move in here with me."

"Ha! As much as I appreciate the offer, I'm not sure I could handle living in a haunted house full-time." Mia shuddered at the thought, though a playful glint sparkled in her dark eyes. "I've got enough ghosts in my head, I don't need to share a bathroom with them."

"Or," Riley teased, unable to resist, "you're just worried about a repeat performance with Lila Rose."

A flush crept up Mia's cheeks, but she chuckled nevertheless. "That too," she admitted, her gaze momentarily drifting towards the ceiling, thinking about her shared moment with the ghost in the attic.

A comfortable silence filled the room for a moment, the two women lost in thought and exhaustion.

"Remember when you came into the bookstore?" Mia asked softly, her voice like a whispered song. "You were so scared."

Riley chuckled at the memory, her eyes crinkling at the corners. "I was a mess, complete and utter disaster." she admitted, her gaze drifting towards the window, as if searching for the person she'd once been.

"And now you've come so far," Mia said gently, her words weighted with admiration. "You stood up to Mason Blackwood all on your own, Riley. That's huge. I've dealt with demons less scary than him."

Riley smiled, considering Mia's words. "Speaking of growth... I remember when you had that panic attack after sensing the malevolence in this house," Riley said, her eyebrows raised in a teasing manner but her tone sincere. "And now, look at you – taking control of your powers and going 'nuclear' like it's nothing."

"Oh that was not 'nothing,'" Mia laughed. "That was in fact the most difficult spell I've ever performed. I am in no way doing that again unless I have to."

"I guess what's important is that we now know we *can* do this stuff when we have to," Riley murmured. "That when it comes down to it, we can rely on ourselves and each other."

"If there's one thing I can promise it's that you can always rely on me, Riley Whittaker," Mia smiled as she felt Riley lean her head on on her side.

"Never thought I'd be so grateful for a friendly shoulder," Riley mumbled sleepily.

Mia chuckled softly, her own fatigue evident in the slight tremor in her voice. "Neither did I, but here we are."

Riley's breathing slowed, her chest rising and falling in rhythm with Mia's as she drifted off to sleep. Her peaceful snores filled the quiet room. The tension that had plagued Riley's face the entire time Mia had known her seemed to finally leave entirely.

Mia's thoughts turned to the power that had surged through her during their confrontation with the vengeful spirit. For the first time in years, Mia had tapped into the full extent of her abilities without succumbing to the dark temptations that had once consumed her. It was a victory in itself, one that she could not have achieved without Riley by her side.

Riley shifted in her sleep, her head nestled more securely against Mia's shoulder. She didn't love Riley the way that she had loved Sarah, but she felt like she could trust this woman just as much. Trust didn't come easily to Mia, and it was nice to no longer feel so alone.

"Riley," Mia whispered, her voice barely audible over the howling autumn wind against the side of the house, "I can't thank you enough for trusting me and letting me into your life during all this... madness."

As if in response to Mia's heartfelt words, Riley stirred from her sleep, her eyelids fluttering open to reveal the clear blue of her eyes. A soft smile graced spread across her face.

"Hey, don't mention it," Riley murmured, her voice thick with sleep. "I wouldn't have made it through any of this without your strength. You've been there for me every step of the way."

Mia smiled in return, her fingers absentmindedly playing with a strand of Riley's golden hair. "Riley," Mia began hesitantly, her voice a low murmur that echoed softly through the quiet room. "I was thinking about Lila."

"Yeah?" Riley replied groggily. "What about her?"

"She told me the one thing she wanted when she was alive was to get out of this house," Mia said, looking up thoughtfully. "And while she's no longer being taunted by Blackwood anymore, she's still stuck here. Her body's still in that attic wall."

"Yeah, that kind of sucks," Riled nodded, still leaning against Mia's side.

"What if we could do something about that?"

Chapter 18

The dim light of the setting sun filtered through the cobweb-laced window as Mia and Riley entered the attic with a sense of hopeful determination. Riley's grip on the sledgehammer was firm but relaxed, the weight of the tool a reminder of the weight of their mission.

As they surveyed the dusty space, Lila almost seemed to shimmer into view before them, her slinky red dress clinging to her delicate frame in the fading light. Her eyes held a seductive glint, yet there was an undeniable sadness lingering in their depths. The spirit that had once terrified Riley that late night looked so vulnerable now.

"I want to thank you, Lila," Riley breathed, her voice quivering with gratitude. "I don't know what would've happened if you hadn't intervened when Mason attacked me."

"I'd like to say I did it for you, Riley," Lila murmured, her voice as soft as silk. "I didn't want you to get hurt, especially not by that monster. But I think I did it for myself more than anything."

Lila's gaze shifted to Mia, her fingers reaching out to brush against the witch's cheek. It was a gesture so tender and intimate that it sent visible shivers down Mia's spine.

Mia turned to meet Lila's eyes. "Thank you, Lila," Mia whispered, swallowing the lump in her throat.

"Why are you sad, beautiful girl," Lila replied, a melancholy smile playing on her lips. "You succeeded in driving off the darkness. You saved all of us here."

"Because I don't think I've done enough," Mia said quietly.

"Enough?" Lila laughed, placing her hand on Mia's arm. "You're the only living thing I've been able to touch in almost a hundred years. You gave me more joy and warmth than I've felt in my entire existence up here."

Lila leaned in and gave Mia a gentle kiss, their arms wrapping around each other. Lila's hands began to roam Mia's body, and Mia let out a low moan.

"I am... still here," Riley said, attempting not to watch. "Just holding a big hammer. Yep. One hundred percent still in the room."

"Sorry Riley, sorry..." Mia said hastily, pulling away from Lila. Her cheeks were flushed, and Lila gave a wry smile.

"Would you... would you like to be laid to rest, Lila?" Riley asked hesitantly, her grip on the sledgehammer shifting as she struggled to find the right words. "To be free?"

Lila looked at her for a long moment, her gaze wistful and filled with longing. "Yes," she whispered finally, her voice quivering with emotion. "All I've ever wanted for as long as I can remember is my freedom."

"Alright then," Riley replied, determination steeling her voice. "We have an idea that we think might work."

With a deep breath, she raised the sledgehammer. Her heart pounding in her chest, the sound echoing in her ears like the beat of a funeral dirge. This was it – if this worked it would be the moment when she would bring an end to Lila's suffering.

Riley swung the hammer, its weight connecting with the wall, and the impact reverberated through Riley's body like the aftershocks of an earthquake. The attic was suddenly filled with a choking cloud of dust and debris. Riley coughed, shielding her face from the swirling particles and squinting through the haze. As the air began to clear, she could see the gaping hole she had created in the wall.

Riley swung the hammer again and again, until most of the plaster was gone, and the hidden chamber was fully revealed.

"Riley, look," Mia breathed, stepping closer and pointing to the skeletal figure curled up in the narrow space. It was a macabre tableau, Lila's bones entwined in tatters of once-silken fabric, the remnants of her once-vivid red dress now faded and decayed.

"Is...is that really her?" Riley whispered, a shudder of revulsion and pity running down her spine. She couldn't tear her gaze away from the tragic sight – the horror that Lila must have experienced in her final moments.

"Thank you, Riley. Thank you, Mia." The spectral voice of Lila Rose echoed softly through the attic, drawing their attention back to her ghostly form. They watched as Lila seemed to shimmer and fade, bathed in a warm, ethereal glow. "You have no idea how much this means to me."

"Of course, Lila," Mia replied, reaching out to touch the waning spirit, but her fingers merely passed through the insubstantial figure. Even Mia's spells wouldn't let her touch Lila anymore. "You deserve peace."

"Riley..." Lila's gaze fell on the blonde professor, her voice trembling with emotion. "I can never repay you for what you've done for me. You saved me."

"No one should have to endure what you did," Riley murmured, her heart aching for the woman. How many nights had Lila wandered these halls, searching for solace, for release from her eternal prison? And how many more would she have suffered if Riley had never moved into this house?

"Thank you both," Lila repeated, her once-sultry voice now imbued with an almost angelic serenity. As the warm glow surrounding her grew brighter, they could see her face soften, the darkness of her past dissipating like shadows before the dawn. "I can't wait to find out what's out there and see what's next."

"Go in peace, Lila," Mia whispered, tears streaming down her cheeks as she bore witness to the spectral transformation.

"Goodbye," Riley added, her voice trembling with the weight of their shared journey. "And good luck, wherever you may find yourself."

The last remnants of Lila's spirit disappeared, leaving Mia and Riley standing amidst the settling debris. The air grew still, imbued with the bittersweet scent of a chapter closed. They exchanged glances, their eyes shining with a mix of awe and relief.

"Wow," Riley breathed, her gaze transfixed upon the now-empty spot where Lila's spirit had once stood. "That was... incredible."

"That feels like an understatement," Mia agreed, running a hand through her curly hair, as she shared a look of understanding with Riley. "We helped free her. We brought her peace."

"True," Riley nodded, folding her arms across her chest. "But it doesn't change the fact that there's a skeleton in my attic." Her voice wavered ever so slightly, betraying the uncertainty gnawing at the edges of her mind.

"Riley," Mia said gently, placing a comforting hand on her shoulder. "What do you think we should do next?"

"I don't know," Riley admitted, her brow furrowing as she considered their options. "I mean, what do people usually do in situations like this?" She shook her head, her frustration mounting. "Do I just call the cops? Oh shit, I *need* to call the cops. I found a body in my house."

"Crap, that's what we need to do," Mia laughed, her practical nature kicking in, "I was so preoccupied with us releasing Lila's spirit I never even thought about what we'd do with the body."

"There are laws about this sort of thing," Riley smiled. "Oh god, I'm going to have to act freaked out about it or else it will be suspicious!"

"What, are you scared they'll blame you for a murder that happened like a century ago?" Mia replied. "Cops can be dumb, but they're not *that* dumb."

"Alright," Riley acquiesced, her resolve solidifying. "I'll call them. After all, it's not every day you find a skeleton in your attic."

"Definitely not," Mia said with a wry smile, her eyes twinkling as she tried to bring some levity to the situation. "I can see the headline now 'Local University Professor Solves Mystery of Lila Rose.'"

"Well, only part of the mystery. I mean, it's not like we can reveal her killer," Riley laughed. "He literally died himself decades *before* he murdered her."

"True, I guess the conspiracy theorists will still have something to gossip about," Mia smiled. "But, uh... how about you don't mention I was here?" Mia started slowly moving towards the stairs.

"Fine, fine," Riley laughed, pulling out her phone. "I'll call you when I get off the phone."

Chapter 19

The morning sun reflected off the brick facades of Garrity University, casting a warm glow on Riley Whittaker as she walked through its gates. The scent of dew-laden grass filled her nostrils, and she couldn't help but smile. It was incredible how different everything felt now that the haunting had vanished from her life like wisps of fog dissipating in the sunlight. She took a moment to bask in her relief, savoring the sense of normalcy that had been so elusive not long ago.

"Morning, Doctor Whittaker!" called out a young student, breaking her reverie.

Riley turned, her gaze meeting that of the eager freshman who had addressed her. "Ah, good morning, Kelly," she replied, getting her brain back into work-mode as she adjusted the strap of her laptop bag on her shoulder.

"Any clue about what you're covering in class today?" the student asked, her voice tinged with curiosity.

Riley nodded, her blonde hair shimmering in the sunlight. "Absolutely. I've prepared a riveting discussion for our class on the diversity of parliamentary systems."

"I'm actually in your introduction to political theory course?" the student replied.

"Ah, Hope you're ready for a pop quiz then – sorry," Riley laughed. "But I still get the credit for getting your name right."

"Shit," Kelly said. "Are you joking?"

"Nope," Riley shook her head. "Didn't do the reading, huh."

"Well, I've still got two hours!" Kelly waved before jogging off towards the library, leaving Riley feeling fairly amused.

As she entered the building, she passed by some of her colleagues who greeted her with polite smiles and nods. She exchanged pleasantries with them, maintaining a balance of professionalism and polite banter. She was a good twenty years younger than most of the other people in the department, and she had to hold herself to a higher standard to be seen as an equal.

But at least she could finally get a good night's sleep again.

"Riley, that paper you published last month was fascinating," remarked an older woman as they waited for the elevator. "Your use of statistical models in examining voting patterns in non-Presidential election years was incredibly interesting."

"Thank you, Phyllis," she replied, her cheeks flushing with pride. "I'm glad you found it compelling."

In truth Riley didn't think it had been her best work, but Dr. Phyllis Winston was a sucker for a good dataset. It was nice to have her say anything positive at all to Riley, so she internally took the win

After weeks of chaos, her life finally seemed to be getting back to normal.

****

The bell above the door chimed as a gust of wind swept through the aisles of Markov Books, ruffling the pages of the volumes that lined the shelves. Mia instinctively shivered, even though she had an active spell guarding against the cold. The long, curly strands of her black hair danced in the breeze as she headed back to the front of the store to find the customer who entered. Her work at the bookstore brought stability to her life; it was a predictable environment where she could lose herself in the arcane and magical.

"Excuse me," a timid voice called out from behind a towering shelf of spell books, drawing Mia's attention. She navigated her way through the narrow alleys formed by the bookshelves, finally coming face to face with a young woman with mousy brown hair wearing thick-rimmed glasses.

"Can I help you?" Mia asked, her voice a melodic blend of warmth and weariness.

"Um, yes, I'm looking for something on... divination," the young woman stammered, blushing slightly. "But not just the usual stuff you have here up front. Something more... obscure."

"How obscure do you need?" Mia smiled, putting her hand on her hip. "What have you already tried?"

"I was... I was working with a copy of Thomas Meser's Greater Grimoire, but it wasn't getting me anywhere?" the woman said nervously. "Before that I saw some success with Pendle's Variance, but it's only designed for limited use and isn't really adaptable. Is that... do you have Fragnelli's sigil of power on your right leg?"

Mia glanced down, and smiled. "Yes, yes I do. All of my tattoos are sigils."

"You can do that?" the young woman asked nervously.

"There are many things you can do, you just have to think to try them," Mia said with a wink. "Now about your request... I think I might have just the thing."

She led the young woman deeper into the shadowy recesses of the store, past rows of mass produced witchcraft books and tarot decks. They arrived at a darker corner of Zelda's store, where the stranger books most customers would overlook were kept.

"Here we are," Mia said, stopping before a section dedicated to divination. She reached for a small, unassuming leather bound book tucked away between larger, more ostentatious tomes. "Sounds like you've been sticking with ceremonial magicians, and some of their frames of reference don't adapt well in the modern age. If Meser's giving you issues, I think we need a different tack. This one's a rare find – it's a copy of the journals of Cassandra Abignail. She was a folk magic practitioner who lived during the 17th century. She experimented with various forms of divination that were considered taboo at the time. A small press in Wales published copies of it in the 1960s. Just a warning, she can get a bit... sexually explicit? Either skip or make sure you read pages forty-seven through sixty-five depending on what you think about that sort of thing."

"Wow," the young woman breathed, her eyes widening as she carefully took the book from Mia's hands. "Thank you so much! I never would have found this on my own."

Mia smiled, a mixture of satisfaction and melancholy flickering across her features. "It's my pleasure. I hope it serves you well."

As the young woman retreated to a quiet corner of the store to peruse her newfound treasure, Mia remained among the stacks, her mind wandering to the darker corners of her own past. Temptation was never going to go away.

The desire for demonic possession would always be with her, but there was so much more to the power she could wield. She could help people and make a difference, from people like Riley desperate for help to young witches needing guidance.

And sharing what she knew and providing that guidance was more fulfilling than she'd ever imagined.

Lost in thought, Mia absently traced one of the protective sigils tattooed on her body, reminders of the darker times she had left behind, but also hopeful for her future.

"Hey, Mia," said a voice so monotonous it almost blended into the background noise of the creaking wooden bookshelves. Mike, her manager, approached her with all the enthusiasm of a man walking to his own execution. "We need to discuss restocking the crystals."

"Of course," Mia replied, her patience shining through as she stifled a sigh. Mike had a talent for making even the most interesting topics feel like a chore. She followed him to the back room, where rows of cardboard boxes filled with quartz, amethyst, and other stones awaited them.

"Inventory shows we're low on citrine and rose quartz. Zelda wants us to check the inventory. I need you to count what we have left and then update the system," Mike droned, handing her a clipboard and pen.

"Got it," she said, forcing a smile. As Mike retreated to the office, Mia took a deep breath and tried to find some enjoyment in the mundane task. Each crystal held its own unique energy, and she focused on the sensation of their vibrations as she handled them, allowing herself a brief respite from the anesthetic effect of Mike's presence.

As she finished counting the last of the rose quartz, she glanced over at a small wooden box nestled in the corner of the shelf. A mischievous grin spread across her face as she lifted the lid, revealing a collection of shining black crystals, each with a small sigil on them. Something was bound into them, but Mia wasn't sure what.

"I wonder..." she mused, her heart quickening with anticipation.

Mia selected two of the stones, feeling their cool, smooth surface against her fingertips. She closed her eyes, focusing her intent on them, and whispered an incantation under her breath. A shiver ran down her spine as the obsidian seemed to pulse in response to her words, its energy resonating with hers. Clicking the two stones together sent a ripple of energy through her body. Mia let out a small noise of surprise.

"Everything okay back here?" Mike's voice cut through the charged atmosphere like a dull knife through butter. Mia quickly tucked the crystals back into their box, hiding it from view.

"Yep, all good," she replied, her pulse still racing from the brief brush with the stones. "Just finishing up with the crystals. We need to put these ones behind the counter. We shouldn't let anyone buy from this particular set unless they ask for them specifically."

"Great," Mike said, seemingly oblivious to the hidden excitement that had just transpired. "Once you're done, I need you to dust the shelves in the front."

"Of course," Mia agreed, stifling a groan. As she carried on with her tasks, she allowed herself to savor the small moments of pleasure she found in her work: the energy of the crystals, the secrets held within the ancient texts, and the brief encounters with the curious souls she could help guide if they asked.

For now, these moments would have to be enough. But deep down, Mia knew that her drive for the arcane could

never truly be exhausted – not even by the crushing
boredom generator named Mike.

Chapter 20

Mia sat hunched in her small apartment over her cluttered desk, the dim light of her one lamp casting shadows across her furrowed brow. Her laptop lay closed in front of her, its sleek surface taunting her with the possibilities it held within. The room was silent except for the occasional rumble of traffic outside and the erratic beating of her own heart. It had been a year since she last talked to Sarah, but the woman lived rent free in her head. There wasn't a day that went by where she didn't wish Sarah was beside her.

"Come on, Graves," she muttered, trying to infuse her voice with a touch of that old sarcastic confidence. "You've faced down ghosts and demons. You almost ripped a hole in yourself channeling unimaginable magic. You can handle searching for your ex online." But even as she heard herself say the words, she realized that real ghosts were far less scary than the metaphoric ones she was tackling.

With a deep breath, she opened her laptop, its eerie glow illuminating her face as it sprang to life. Her hands trembled ever so slightly as she navigated to various social media sites, her heartbeat racing faster with each click. She hesitated for a moment, her fingers hovering above the keyboard, before typing Sarah's name into the search bar.

"I'm just looking," Mia told herself. "There's nothing wrong with looking. She'll never know that I looked."

As the results appeared on screen, Mia's eyes darted between the dozens of profiles for different women named "Sarah Masters." Mia's pulse pounded in her ears like a drumbeat as she continued to scroll through accounts. And then, there she was.

Sarah's familiar face stared back at her from the screen, her intense brown eyes piercing through Mia's defenses.

"Hi Sarah," Mia whispered, her voice a mixture of awe and trepidation. "You always knew how to make an entrance."

The image of Sarah's face seemed to beckon her like a siren's call. Mia's finger trembled as it hovered above the trackpad, before finally giving in to the magnetic pull of Sarah's profile picture. The click seemed to echo through the room like a gunshot, and Mia found herself holding her breath as the page loaded.

"And you're just there, still existing," Mia whispered under her breath, as the first image that greeted her was a recent photo of Sarah standing on a rooftop, arms outstretched towards the sky, her long chestnut hair was cut short, dancing around her face like a halo. Her smile was wide and genuine, a sight Mia had not seen for years.

"God, you look so happy," she murmured, her heart clenching with a potent mixture of longing, regret, and curiosity. She scrolled through Sarah's posts, each one more enigmatic than the last. Cryptic quotes about strength and perseverance accompanied photos of sunsets, shadowy alleyways, and the occasional selfie.

"Come on, Sarah. Give me something to work with," Mia muttered, her frustration mounting as she tried to decipher the hidden meaning behind her ex's digital breadcrumb trail. It felt as if Sarah was deliberately keeping her life shrouded in mystery, an impenetrable fortress that no unwanted visitor could breach.

"Of course, she wouldn't make this easy for me," Mia thought ruefully, remembering how stubborn and secretive Sarah could be.

As she delved further into the online labyrinth, Mia's thoughts were flooded with memories of the years they spent together – finding each other on the streets of Boston, two lost teenagers with no one else to turn to. They did so many things Mia wasn't proud of, but they survived – and in some ways thrived.

Mia couldn't help but smile as she remembered the first time they kissed, in the back alley behind the diner where Mia was working after having convinced the creep of an owner to pay her under the table. It had been a hot summer night, and they had both been drenched in sweat from the sweltering heat. It was awkward and neither knew what they were doing, but it was wonderful.

They were so innocent and naive. If only the years had let them stay that way.

Mia pulled herself out of her memories, and went back to looking through Sarah's social media. Most of Sarah's photos were from her workouts, showcasing her muscular frame that seemed sculpted from marble. Mia couldn't help but stare, her own body responding to the sight of Sarah's toned arms and abs with a familiar, primal hunger.

"Wow Sarah… what a difference a year makes," she thought, her fingers twitching with the urge to reach out to Sarah, to bridge the chasm that had grown between since Mia left.

Her cursor hovered over the message button, a digital lifeline that could reconnect her to the woman who had once consumed her every waking thought for over ten years. But as she hesitated, the weight of their shared past threatened to crush her, and she found herself questioning whether reopening old wounds was the right thing to do.

"Is it worth the risk?" she whispered, her voice barely audible over the hum of the computer's fan. "Would reaching out to Sarah unearth those demons for the both of us?"

Sarah had lost so much because of Mia. Half of Sarah's soul was gone because of her. If she had managed to move on and find a new happiness without Mia, didn't she owe letting Sarah have that?

This was selfish. Mia realized she was just thinking about her own needs, and her own desires. Mia wanted forgiveness, but it could cost Sarah whatever joy she'd found in the process of getting it. Mia had taken more from Sarah than she could ever repay.

She refused to take anything else.

Mia closed the browser window and shut down her laptop. *I'm letting you go Sarah. I'm letting you go.*

About the Author

Trae Dorn is just your average geeky, nonbinary genderqueer witch. They live just on the edge of the woods somewhere in Wisconsin with their spouse.

They are the creator of the comics UnCONventional and Peregrine Lake. They also run the Nerd & Tie Podcast Network where they host a number of shows including the popular witchcraft podcast BS-Free Witchcraft.

They are also very, very tired.

You can find more about them at **traedorn.com**